# Th

# I

# The Case of the Lazy Lover

## Erle Stanley Gardner

G.K. Hall & Co. • Chivers Press
Thorndike, Maine USA  Bath, England

This Large Print edition is published by G.K. Hall & Co., USA and by Chivers Press, England.

Published in 1998 in the U.S. by arrangement with Thayer Hobson & Company.

Published in 1998 in the U.K. by arrangement with Thayer Hobson & Company.

U.S.  Softcover  0-7838-8348-X (Paperback Collection Edition)
U.K.  Hardcover 0-7540-3171-3 (Chivers Large Print)
U.K.  Softcover  0-7540-3172-1 (Camden Large Print)

The text of this Large Print edition is unabridged.
Other aspects of the book may vary from the original edition.

Set in 16 pt. Plantin by Juanita Macdonald.

Printed in the United States on permanent paper.

**British Library Cataloguing in Publication Data available**

**Library of Congress Cataloging in Publication Data**

Gardner, Erle Stanley, 1889–1970.
    The case of the lazy lover / Erle Stanley Gardner.
        p.      cm.
    ISBN 0-7838-8348-X (lg. print : sc : alk. paper)
    1. Mason, Perry (Fictitious character) — Fiction.
    2. Large type books.   I. Title.
    [PS3513.A6322L39    1998]
    813′.52—dc21
                                                    97-38563

# The Case of the Lazy Lover

# Cast Of Characters

PERRY MASON — a criminal lawyer with a steel-trap mind and a stubborn desire to get at the truth

DELLA STREET — Perry Mason's confidential secretary

LOLA FAXON ALLRED — the attractive, middle-aged wife of Bertrand C. Alfred. She is — more than she suspects — at a dangerous age

BERTRAND C. ALLRED — a powerful mine operator with a ruthless resolve to get what he wants

GERTIE — Perry Mason's plump, good-natured receptionist, who displays an unsuspected talent for drama

ROBERT GREGG FLEETWOOD — Bertrand C. Allred's right-hand man, who disappears with Mrs. Allred under mysterious circumstances

PATRICIA FAXON — Mrs. Allred's daughter by a prior marriage, a beautiful damsel in distress

JOHN BAGLEY — a leading contender for Patricia Faxon's affections

GEORGE JEROME — Allred's partner in mining deals. A clever man — perhaps as clever as Allred

DIXON KEITH — he swapped mining properties with Allred and Jerome — and learned a bitter lesson

MERVIN CANBY — president of the Farmers, Merchants & Mechanics Bank, who is busy with checks and double checks

PAUL DRAKE — head of the Drake Detective Agency. Thanks to Perry Mason, he does much sleuthing and little sleeping

C. E. PAWLING — president of the First National Bank at Las Olitas, who is distressed at the financial antics of an important depositor

MAURINE MILFORD — an extremely attractive young woman who leaves an extremely puzzling trail

JANE SMITH — the description matched, but the name didn't

FRANK INMAN — a treat-'em-rough investigator from the sheriff's office

LIEUTENANT TRAGG — a homicide-squad officer who, he thinks, has outsmarted Perry Mason

P. E. OVERBROOK — an expert on back-tracking — in more ways than one

BERNICE ARCHER — Fleetwood's girl friend. Her figure is remarkable — and so is her I.Q.

LEIGHTON — a service station operator. The phone call wasn't finished, but the alibi was

BERT HUMPHREYS — his diagram was carefully plotted — and so was the witness's story

D. T. DANVERS — the Assistant District Attorney, who has a passion for details but overlooks a crucial point

JUDGE COLTON — he disapproved of fishing expeditions — and then Perry Mason pulled in a whopper

# Chapter 1

There was usually a big pile of mail on Monday morning. Della Street, Perry Mason's confidential secretary, having arrived a full half hour before the office was scheduled to open, deftly inserted the paper knife under the flaps of the envelopes, cut them open with one swift wrist motion, read the letters and sorted them into three piles.

First, there was the pile that Perry Mason must read and answer. The second pile didn't require an immediate answer, but called for Mason's attention. The third pile was mail which she would discuss with Mason, but which she, herself, could handle.

The last envelope she owned was the one which presented the puzzle. It was a thin envelope and might have contained merely a routine statement of accounts covering some purchases Mason had made. Actually, it held a folded oblong of tinted paper with serrated edges. The body was typewritten, the signature in heavy ink.

Della Street saw that it was a check drawn on the Farmers, Merchants & Mechanics Bank for two thousand five hundred dollars, payable to Perry Mason and signed *Lola Faxon Allred*.

Della shook the envelope to make certain nothing else was in it; then, to make certain that her memory was not at fault, consulted the card index of Mason's clients.

There was no one named Allred.

It might, of course, be conscience money, so Della Street went to the big master file.

In this file, there was a record of every person with whom Perry Mason had had a business contact, witnesses in cases, persons who had served on juries in cases that Mason had tried, persons who had been in an adverse business position, defendants in civil actions, parties to contracts, hostile witnesses.

There was no Allred.

Della Street was just closing the drawer when Mason came breezing into the office.

"Hi, Della. What's new? The usual assortment of mail, I see. Gosh, how I like to get letters! And how I hate to answer them!"

Della Street said, "Who's Lola Faxon Allred?"

"You've got me," Mason said, after thinking a moment. "Were you looking for her in the file?"

"Uh huh."

"Find anything?"

"Not a thing."

"Why the interest?"

Della Street said, "She sent you a check for twenty-five hundred bucks."

"For what?"

"She didn't say."

"No letter?"

"No letter."

"And we have nothing in the files?"

"No."

Mason said, "Let's take a look at the check."

He studied it for a moment, turned it so that the light from the office window struck the check diagonally, said, "You're sure there wasn't any letter in the envelope, Della?"

"Absolutely. This is the envelope, Chief. This is just the way it came."

Mason said, "Originally, there was a letter attached to this check."

"How do you know?"

Mason said, "The way it's folded, for one thing. For another thing, the fact that there is the mark of a paper clip on the top of the check. Hold it at just this angle, Della. No, a little more that way. That's it. Now see how the faint indentation in the paper shows the outline of a paper clip?"

"That's right," Della said. "A clip was there, all right. What makes you think it was clipped to a letter?"

"The way the check is folded. If you were putting a check in an envelope, you'd fold it once. When a check is attached to a letter, you clip it to the top of the letter, then you fold the letter once from the bottom, then you fold it twice from the sides. That is, you fold it once from each side. Now notice the way this check is folded. Once from the left, once from the right."

"Then what do you suppose became of the letter?"

Mason said, "That's the question, Della. Look

13

in the phone book."

Della Street ran her finger down the "A's" in the phone book, said, "I don't find any Lola Faxon Allred. There's a Bertrand C. Allred."

"Bertrand C.!" Mason exclaimed.

"Yes. Why? Do you know him?"

"Well, I know *of* him."

"What about him, Chief?"

"He's a big shot in mining circles. He's both a promoter and operator. He has the reputation of being clever and tricky. A year or so ago he promoted a mine. After he'd sold the stock there was a discovery of very rich ore. Allred used a slick legal trick to get the stock back. He made a million."

"Slick legal tricks interest me," Della said. "How did he do it?"

"He had a friendly stockholder, who was really a dummy, sue him for fraud, claim the stock was valueless and ask for his money back. Then this dummy sent out letters to all of the other stockholders, stating that the suit had been filed, that Allred had promoted the mine by fraudulent means, that if the other stockholders wanted to take concerted action, the writer felt it would be possible to salvage *all* of their money; but that Allred would undoubtedly try to spar for time, so that he could dissipate the company assets. Two days later, Allred wrote each and every one of the stockholders telling them that, in *his* opinion, the mine was fabulously rich; that new discoveries had greatly enhanced the value of the stock; that every share of stock that had been sold was not treasury stock but Allred's private stock; that he wanted the investors to make a lot of money out of it and his advice was to sit tight and not try to make him give them their money back; that, in his opinion, the mine was even more valuable than when he had sold them the stock.

"You can see the effect such a letter would have. It made the stockholders feel they could get their money back if they took concerted action. You sell a man stock in a mining company and then go and try to *buy* the stock back, and he wants at least ten times what he paid for it. You offer him exactly what he paid for it, and he laughs in your face; but if you tell him there's a possibility, that by taking prompt action, he can *'get his money back,'* those words are music to his ears. He wants his money back.

"Well, the upshot of it was that Allred bought back nearly all of the stock at exactly what he'd sold it for. Later on, when some of the stockholders claimed they'd been whipsawed, Allred simply produced the letter he'd written them stating that in his opinion the mine was fabulously rich, that there had been recent discoveries which enhanced his faith in the mine. In other words, he had written them this letter telling them the entire truth, begging them and imploring them not to ask him to refund their money. Of course, the moral effect of the letter was to make them fall all over themselves trying to get the money back, but the legal effect was that Allred had made a complete disclosure of all of the facts in the case."

15

"He must be clever," Della Street said.

"He's slick," Mason told her. "Are there any other Allreds?"

"No Allreds who seem to have a street address that fits in with twenty-five hundred dollar checks."

Mason said, "Just on the off-chance, Della, get Allred's residence on the wire."

"For whom shall I ask?"

Mason hesitated a moment, then said, "I'll do the talking. Dial the number for me, Della, then I'll take over."

Della Street got an outside line. Her trained fingers whirled the dial with swift precision. She nodded to Mason and said, "I've dialed."

Mason picked up his telephone, waited.

A moment later, a feminine voice said, "Hello. Mr. Allred's residence."

"Is Mrs. Allred there?" Mason asked.

"Who wishes to speak with her please?"

"Mr. Perry Mason, the lawyer."

"Was she expecting you to call, Mr. Mason?"

Mason laughed and said, "That depends. Tell me, is her full name Lola Faxon Allred?"

"That's right," the voice at the other end of the line said.

"I think, then," Mason said, "you may say that she's expecting me to call."

"Hold the line a moment, please."

Mason held the line for some ten seconds, then a masculine voice said, "Hello, Mr. Mason."

"Yes."

16

"This is Bertrand C. Allred. You wish to talk with my wife?"

"Yes."

"She isn't here at the moment."

"I see."

"Could you tell me what it was that — that is, the general nature of what you wish to discuss with her? I may be able to get in touch with her a little later on."

"Nothing important," Mason said. "Just tell her I called, if you will."

"I'll do that, but if you could perhaps tell me . . ."

"I'm just checking up on something," Mason said. "That's all. You might convey that message to your wife, if you will, that I was checking — just *checking,* and that I'd like to have her call me in connection with that check. Got that? Thanks very much."

"On what," Allred asked, "are you checking?"

"A routine matter," Mason said. "And thank you *very* much indeed, Mr. Allred. Good-by."

He hung up the telephone and glanced at Della Street. "I may have put my foot in it. Her husband got on the phone. He's curious. I wish I knew what was in the letter that had originally been clipped to that check."

"Did he show too much interest?" Della Street asked.

"Yes. We'll now play a waiting game for a while."

"And the check?"

17

"We'll just hold it and see what happens."

"And the mail?"

Mason said with a note of surrender in his voice, "Oh, all right, I suppose I'll have to wade through it. Get your notebook, Della, and let's start."

At nine-forty a special delivery letter was relayed to Della Street's desk through the hands of Gertie, the receptionist in the outer office. Della Street opened it. The thin envelope contained only a single sheet of paper, a tinted oblong of paper.

This check was folded squarely in the middle, just as Mason had said a check would have been folded if there had been no letter accompanying it, and was drawn on the First National Bank at Las Olitas. The check was payable to Perry Mason, was in an amount of twenty-five hundred dollars and was signed *Lola Faxon Allred.*

The letter had been postmarked early that morning.

Della Street said, "Your girl friend has a strange idea of confetti. I wonder how long this is going to keep up."

"Both checks dated Saturday?" Mason asked.

"That's right."

"Do we have an account at the Farmers, Merchants & Mechanics Bank ourselves?" Mason mused.

"Of course."

Mason said, "Go down to the bank, deposit both checks. Ask the cashier to pay particular attention to them, and when he sends the check through for collection on the First National Bank at Las Olitas, to ask the bank there to check carefully."

"Will you be under any obligation to Mrs. Allred if you accept these checks without knowing what they're for?"

"I can always give her back the money, if I decide not to represent her in whatever matter it is she wants me to handle. Go down to the bank personally, Della, and put the checks through. There's something about this that I definitely don't like."

"I like it," Della said, smiling. "As the one who handles the finances of this office, I'll be only too pleased to have Mrs. Allred pelt us with checks by every mail. Why don't *you* like it, Chief?"

"I don't know. Call it a hunch if you like, but I have an idea that when I deposit these checks, things are going to start happening — and that that's the reason the checks are being sent. Let's co-operate and see what happens after that."

# Chapter 2

Della Street had a report for Mason by ten-twenty.

"We gave the cashier at the Farmers, Merchants & Mechanics Bank a jolt," she said.

"How come?"

"He couldn't understand why we would be depositing a check and at the same time asking him to examine it carefully."

"But he scrutinized it carefully?"

"Yes."

"And passed it?"

"Said the check was unquestionably good, that it was signed by Mrs. Allred and that Mrs. Allred had ample funds to cover it. He didn't even bother about checking balances. He only checked signatures. Mrs. Allred must have a pretty big account there."

Mason said, "The thing interests me. Mrs. Allred certainly should be getting in touch with me — unless the checks are phony."

"Probably," Della Street said, "she folded that first check in a letter explaining what she wanted you to do, then she remembered something else she wanted to add to the letter, took it out to put a postscript on it and then overlooked putting it back in the envelope. The check remained in the envelope and came through all right."

"I suppose so," Mason admitted, "but the darn thing irritates me. I . . ."

The phone on Della Street's desk sounded in a single short, quick ring, indicating that the receptionist in the outer office had a matter which she wished to take up directly with Mason's secretary.

Della Street picked up the phone, said, "Hello, Gertie. What is it . . . I see . . . Yes, I think so. Ask him to be seated for just a moment."

Della Street cupped her hand over the mouthpiece of the telephone, said to Mason, "Mr. Bertrand C. Allred is out there. He seems to be quite worked up about something. He wants to see you, but won't say why."

Mason grinned and said, "Now we're getting somewhere! Tell Gertie to bring him in."

Bertrand C. Allred was around fifty, a short, stocky individual, wearing a double-breasted gray suit that had been carefully tailored to make him appear to the best advantage. His hair, thin at the top, was parted in the middle, plastered down on a scalp which showed through the thin, reddish-brown locks. A stubby red mustache, close cropped, shadowed his upper lip but stopped before it came to the corners of his mouth, a mere half-inch of short, carefully scissored hair on each side of the upper lip.

He was, quite apparently, a man who, relying upon the power of personality to blast any obstacle out of his way, smashed his way through life as a varsity ball carrier crashes through the opposition of a scrub team.

Allred's pudgy legs drove him across Mason's office. His face wreathed in a cordial smile, he extended his hand when he was still six feet from the lawyer's desk. He said in a booming voice, "Perry Mason! Perry Mason, in person! This is indeed a treat! Mr. Mason, I've heard a great deal about you. I'm very, very, very glad to meet you."

"Thank you," Mason said, shaking hands. "Won't you be seated?"

Allred looked meaningly toward Della Street.

"Miss Street, my secretary," Mason explained. "You may trust her discretion absolutely. She takes notes on conversations, keeps things straight for me and supplements my recollection when my memory is at fault."

"I don't suppose that's very often," Allred boomed.

"Sometimes I trip up on details," Mason admitted.

Allred seated himself in the big leather client's chair, cleared his throat, said, "Mind if I smoke?"

"Not at all," Mason said. "Care for one of these?"

He extended an office humidor of cigarettes.

"No, thank you. Cigarettes just tantalize me. I prefer cigars. No objection?"

"None whatever."

Allred crossed his pudgy legs. His nails, freshly manicured, made glistening reflections of the light from the window as he extracted a cigar from a leather case which he took from his pocket.

"It's about my wife, Mr. Mason."

"What about her?" Mason asked.

"I hardly know how to account for her actions."

Mason said, "Let's not misunderstand each other, Mr. Allred. You are coming here because I phoned and asked to talk with your wife?"

"In a way, but only in a way."

"You must always realize," Mason warned, "that when you talk with an attorney, you may present facts concerning which the lawyer is not free to act."

"You mean you might be representing my wife?"

"I meant that I might not be free to act as your attorney, if that's what you had in mind. Therefore, you should tell me exactly what you want, before divulging any information which you might wish to have considered confidential."

"That's all right. That's all right," Allred said, scraping a match on the sole of a broad shoe, holding the flame to the end of the cigar, puffing nervously while he got the tobacco burning to his satisfaction.

Allred shook the match out, dropped it in the ashtray, said to Mason, "You're representing my wife?"

"I'm not prepared to answer that question at the moment."

"Well, if you are, and it seems that you are, how did it happen that you expected to find her at *my* home?"

"Isn't that the logical place to look for a wife, in the husband's home?"

Allred peered through the blue haze of his cigar smoke to study the lawyer's features. "Damned if you aren't a deep one," he admitted grudgingly, "unless —"

"Unless what?" Mason asked as the other lapsed into silence.

"Unless for some reason you don't know — but if you're representing Lola you *must* know."

Mason merely smiled.

"Oh, what's the use of sparring around like this, Mason? Let's get down to brass tacks."

"Go right ahead."

"My wife," Allred said bitterly, "has run away with my best friend."

"That's too bad," Mason said noncommittally. "When did she leave?"

"As though you didn't know all about it!"

"After all, Mr. Allred, you're the one who sought this interview."

"Saturday night," Allred said. "Damn it, you could have knocked me over with a feather."

"The man's name?"

"Robert Gregg Fleetwood. One of my business associates, an employee, accountant, assistant, handy man."

"Do you intend to apply for a divorce?"

"I don't know."

"I take it the newspapers know nothing of this?"

"Of course not. I've kept it out of the newspa-

24

pers, so far. I can't sit on the lid much longer. We're too well known, socially and otherwise."

Mason's contribution to the conversation was a mere nod.

"What I can't figure," Allred said explosively, "is how a woman her age could do a thing like that!"

"How old is she?"

"Forty-two."

"I believe," Mason said, "that psychologists agree that that is one of the most dangerous ages for a woman."

"You're talking in generalities," Allred said.

"Why not?"

"All right, if you want to — but look here, Mason. Lola had plenty of property; she could do anything she wished. She was a mature woman. If she got tired of me, why didn't she simply go to Reno, discreetly announced that there had been a separation, get her divorce and marry Bob Fleetwood? But no, she had to do something spectacular, something that is almost adolescent, something that will give us a lot of unfavorable publicity."

"Can you tell me anything about Fleetwood?"

"I can tell you everything about him."

"Well?"

"Bob Fleetwood is fifteen years younger than my wife. I picked him up as a young man, and tried to make something of him. I pushed him ahead just as fast as he could go. I trusted him. He was at my home much of the time. Hang it,

I had no idea he and Lola could see anything in each other. Bob Fleetwood was apparently paying court to Patricia."

"And who's Patricia?"

"Patricia Faxon, Lola's daughter by a prior marriage."

"I see."

"And then, all of a sudden, he runs off with my wife."

"What does Pat say about it?"

"She's crying her eyes out, but she pretends she isn't. She comes to meals, eats just enough to keep her alive, puts on a bold front, pretends to be smiling and happy, and is eating her heart out."

"She loves him?"

"I think she's humiliated, more than anything. Puts a girl in a helluva position when her mother runs off with her sweetheart."

"And Fleetwood was Patricia's sweetheart?"

"Well, let's look at it this way. He was . . . He . . . Well, he was around Patricia quite a lot, and during that time he certainly never seemed to take any interest in Lola. They must have been damn clever, or else it was something that just came up all at once.

"Of course, Patricia's a modern girl. She's had swains by the dozen. Lots of them have been crazy about her. Lately the field narrowed down to two, Bob Fleetwood and a chap named John Bagley. I felt Bob had the inside track, but John Bagley was still in the running — make

26

no mistake about that, Mason."

The lawyer nodded.

"I suppose," Allred went on, "that Pat got to playing one against the other, the way a woman will, and went too far. Perhaps she really picked Bagley and gave Bob the mitten. You can't tell."

"Can't you ask her?" Mason inquired.

"Not Pat. She has a mind of her own. She thinks I tried to dominate her and resented it. All a misunderstanding, I can assure you, Mason, but that's the way she feels. Well, anyway, if she did jilt Bob for John, she certainly put *me* in a spot.

"I suppose Bob decided he wanted to show Pat she wasn't the only girl in the world, and he wanted to humiliate her, so he ran off with her mother. Sure puts me in a hell of a spot! But I can't imagine Lola doing anything like that."

Mason merely nodded.

"Hang it all!" Allred went on irritably, "even if Lola didn't give a damn about me, if she wanted to do everything she could to hurt me or to make me ridiculous, you still can't imagine her pulling a trick like that."

"Did she do what she did solely to hurt you, or make you ridiculous?" Mason asked.

"It looks that way, doesn't it?"

Mason remained silent.

"I suppose the only explanation is that Lola had been secretly in love with him for some time. She probably felt that Pat didn't really love him. I suppose she was afraid to tell me she wanted a divorce and wait for the thing to be handled in a decent way, because if she had, Bob would probably have wriggled off her hook. After all, no matter how young looking and attractive a woman is, when she ties up with a man who's fifteen years younger than she is — well, it's only a question of time, Mason. It's only a question of time."

"Exactly what do you want me to do?" Mason asked. "Make comments on your domestic entanglements, or give you information."

"As a matter of fact, I wanted information, Mason."

"So I gathered."

"But only as a preliminary to something else."

"I'm afraid I don't understand."

"I wanted to find out if you were representing my wife. I want a definite answer on that."

"I can't give it to you."

"If you are representing her, I want to establish communication with her."

"She'll get in touch with you, if she wants to, I suppose," Mason said.

"Dammit, it isn't what *she* wants. It's what *I* want."

"Yes?"

"Yes! I want to get Bob Fleetwood."

"And Fleetwood," Mason said, "knowing something of the risks one naturally runs in encountering an irate husband, is equally anxious to keep out of your way."

"That's just the point," Allred said earnestly. "He doesn't need to be afraid of me."

"Perhaps it's not fear. Perhaps just prudence."

"Well, whatever it is, I want him to get in touch with me."

"A desire on your part which he may decide to ignore."

"Look here," Allred said, "I'm going to put some more cards on the table."

"Go right ahead."

"Do you know anything about my business, Mason?"

"I know generally you're in the mining business."

"The mining business," Allred went on, "is the greatest gamble in the world. You buy a prospect. It looks good. You pour money into development work. You think it's going to make you a million dollars. It turns out to be a lemon. You have sunk more money than you can afford. Naturally there's a great temptation to try and unload that, and get at least part of your money out."

Mason nodded.

"On the other hand, you get some little hole in the ground and start scratching around, deciding you're not going to spend very much money on it, and the first thing you know, you've blundered into a lot of rich ore. Do you know George Jerome?"

Mason shook his head.

"He's my partner in quite a few mining deals. Nice chap, has a lot of technical knowledge. A pretty hard man to fool, George Jerome."

"And how does George Jerome enter into the picture?"

"We owned the White Horse Mine. We traded it to Dixon Keith for a mine he owned and a little cash. It was a pretty good trade. What I'd call an even swap."

Mason glanced at his wrist watch.

"I'm only to take up a minute. Only a minute. It all ties in to this problem about my wife," Allred said. "Keith traded properties with his eyes open. He thought he was handing us a lemon. I happened to know that he thought his property wasn't worth a thin dime. That's where we fooled him, thanks very largely to my partner's technical knowledge.

"Well, anyway, the mine we got from Dixon Keith proved to be valuable. The fact is, the vein was pinching out. Keith thought he'd better unload the property. George decided there had been a fault, and that Keith had missed the main vein. Well, anyway, George opened up the drift in a different direction, and within three weeks after we'd taken possession, we struck it rich — that is, pretty rich.

"We tried to keep the thing a secret, but in some way it leaked out. Keith got wind of it, and naturally he was furious. The best thing he could do was to try and rescind the contract, put the swap back to where it had been at the start. So he claimed we'd misrepresented *our* property to him and said that he wanted a rescission of the contract. Naturally, we told him to go jump in the lake."

"And what did he do?" Mason asked.

"Got a lawyer and started suit, claiming we were guilty of fraudulent misrepresentations and we hadn't told him about this, that, and the other, that he had relied on our word and hadn't ever made an investigation of the property in person. Now that's a lie, Mason. Dixon Keith went out to that property. He looked it over. He made a thorough study of it and even if we had given him any information, which we didn't, he wouldn't have relied on it.

"The law of fraud, as I understand it, is that if a man relies on false representations, that's one thing; but if he makes an independent investigation and buys the property as the result of that independent investigation, his hands are tied."

"That, generally, is the law," Mason said. "There are, of course, certain exceptions . . ."

"I know, I know, but I'm not talking about the exceptions now. I'm talking about the law. Because this case is dead open and shut. It's a plain case of a man trying to back out of a contract."

"Can you prove Keith went out to inspect your property?" Mason asked.

"Now then, there's the whole point of the matter," Allred admitted. "There's only one person who can prove that."

"Who?"

"Robert Gregg Fleetwood," Allred said bitterly. "The man who has run off with my wife."

"The situation," Mason said, smiling faintly, "would seem to be complicated."

"It is complicated — it's annoying — it's embarrassing. I picked Fleetwood up and made something of him. He's a lazy, no-good. He's run off with my wife, and now he's jeopardizing a lawsuit because no one knows where to get in touch with him. Dixon Keith evidently knows what's up. He's trying to rush the case on for immediate trial. He wants to take my deposition. He wants to take my partner, George Jerome's, deposition. We're in a fix, Mason. We don't want to rely on the claim that he used his independent judgment and made a trip to inspect the White Horse claim, unless we can prove it. You try to depend on something in a lawsuit and then fall down on the proof — well, you're a lawyer yourself. You know how that goes."

"And exactly what," Mason asked, "do you want me to do? I'm not in a position to represent you in your mining litigation."

"I understand all that. We have a lawyer."

"Then what do you want me to do?"

"Look here," Allred said, "you're my wife's lawyer. You can hedge around all you want to. I *know* that you're her lawyer. I want you to get in touch with her."

"What makes you think that I can get in touch with her?"

"I feel confident you can. I want you to tell her that I wish she'd grow up and act her age. Tell her to go to Reno and get a divorce, and it will be all right as far as I'm concerned. And I want you to get in touch with Fleetwood through her and tell Bob Fleetwood to come back and be a man, live up to his responsibilities. If Lola wants him, he can have her. I'm going to play fair with him. I don't think it was his fault entirely. I want to win that lawsuit! I want Bob Fleetwood here and I want him available as a witness. Is that clear?"

"That seems to be quite clear."

Allred heaved himself up out of the chair. "That's all I have to say then."

"And suppose I should not be your wife's attorney?"

"You are."

"But suppose I should not be?"

"Well, I don't know that it makes any difference, one way or another. I've told you what I have to say. I hope I can get in touch with my wife. You know how I feel and you know what to do about it."

"I'm afraid," Mason said, "there's not very much I *can* do about it."

"You have this message to transmit to your client. It's to her advantage to have that message transmitted. I feel sure that you'll do it. Good morning, Mr. Mason."

Allred started back toward the door through which he had entered, then saw the exit door to the corridor, made an abrupt half turn, jerked the door open and barged out of the room without even looking back.

Mason glanced at Della Street.

"Well," she said, "that explains it. Mrs. Allred

wants you to represent her. She evidently wrote you a letter telling you what she'd planned to do and what she wanted you to do, and then —" Della's voice trailed off.

"And then?" Mason demanded.

"Maybe she decided to wait and telephone later on," Della finished weakly.

"You'll have to do better than that, Della," Mason grinned.

# Chapter 3

Ten minutes after Allred had left, Gertie, Mason's receptionist, tiptoed personally into Mason's office to announce in an awed voice, "Gee, Mr. Mason, the bank president's out there."

"Who?" Mason asked.

"Mr. Mervin Canby, president of the Farmers, Merchants & Mechanics Bank. He wants to see you upon a matter he says is confidential."

"Well, send him in," Mason said.

"Right away?"

"Right now!"

"Yes, Mr. Mason. I — well, I thought I'd better tell you instead of telephoning you."

"That's fine, Gertie. Send him in."

Mason and Della Street exchanged glances as Gertie vanished through the door to the outer office.

Mervin Canby, a frosty, gray man with gray hair, gray eyebrows, gray mustache, and gray eyes, had a cordial smile for Della Street, another for Mason. But there was no great warmth about him, and his manner indicated quite plainly that he was calling upon a serious matter of business.

"Sit down," Mason invited.

Canby settled himself in the chair, said, "I'll come directly to the point, Mr. Mason. I'm a busy man and I know you're a busy man."

Mason nodded.

"You deposited two checks with us, Mr. Mason. One of them was on our bank, was in your favor in an amount of twenty-five hundred dollars and signed by Lola Faxon Allred."

Mason said nothing, waiting for the banker to go on.

"The other check," Canby said, "was drawn on the First National Bank of Las Olitas. That too was in your favor. That too was in an amount of twenty-five hundred dollars.

"When you deposited those checks," Canby said, "you asked the cashier to examine them with great care."

"Miss Street did that," Mason said.

"May I ask, Mr. Mason, if that was at your suggestion?"

"It was."

"Why?"

"Because I wanted to make certain the checks were good."

"That is hardly a customary practice."

"Perhaps not."

"Did you have some reason to believe those checks were not in order?"

"That's a difficult question to answer. Suppose you tell me first why you're here."

Canby said, "The cashier kept thinking things over. After you had left he came to me and asked my advice. I examined the checks and then sent for our handwriting expert."

"Isn't *that* rather unusual?" Mason asked.

"I found something on one of the checks which puzzled me," Canby said. "I wanted to have my judgment checked by a professional. Of course, his opinion at the present moment is more or less tentative — that is, on one check. On the other, the situation is different."

"In what way?"

"The check drawn upon us is apparently signed by Lola Faxon Allred. The check drawn on the First National Bank at Las Olitas is quite possibly forged."

"The deuce, it is!" Mason ejaculated.

"That's right. The forgery can be demonstrated."

"How?"

"By the aid of a microscope. Someone traced the signature on the check with a piece of carbon paper. That's one of the oldest forms of forgery known and a modification of the tracing formula. A person gets a paper bearing the genuine signature of the one whose name he wants to forge. He puts a sheet of carbon paper under that signature and the document which is to be forged, underneath the carbon paper. Then very gently the forger runs a toothpick or other pointed instrument over the lines of the genuine signature. The pressure is light enough so that it leaves a barely perceptible carbon paper imprint of the signature on the paper beneath."

"Then what?" Mason asked.

"Then the forger takes a pen, usually a pen

with a quite heavy ink, such perhaps as black drawing ink, or any India ink."

"Go ahead."

"And traces loop by loop, line by line, over the carbon paper signature. Frankly, Mr. Mason, it makes a most excellent forgery, one, which when skillfully done, can only be detected by an expert — depending somewhat upon the age, the mentality, and the emotions of the person forging the signature. The pen, of course, moves more slowly than in the case of a genuine signature. Therefore, if a person is nervous, there are more apt to be microscopic irregularities in the lines of the signature, due to tremors. But if a person has a steady hand and is free from mental excitement, the forgery can be made quite convincing."

Mason merely nodded.

"The forged check in this instance," Canby went on, "was made either by someone who had passed middle age or someone who was under an emotional tension. While the naked eye shows nothing, the microscope does show very distinct tremor lines."

"Indeed," Mason said.

"So," Canby went on, "I wanted to get in touch with you and find out exactly what you know about that check."

"Why not get in touch with Mrs. Allred?"

"We've tried that. It seems that she is not available at the moment."

"Do you know where she is?"

"She apparently left with friends on a motor

trip. Her husband seems to take her absence very lightly, says that he hasn't the faintest idea where to reach her and won't have until she sends him word from somewhere. He says she went off with some friends of hers who are interested in photography and they're just wandering about."

"Doesn't seem to be the least bit disturbed about her absence?"

Canby looked at Mason sharply. "Any reason why he should?"

Mason said irritably, "Don't try that stuff on me, Canby. My questions are for the purpose of trying to help you. If you're going to adopt that attitude, I'll simply wash my hands of the whole affair."

"Of course, *you* deposited the check," Canby pointed out.

"Certainly, I did," Mason said, "and I'll tell you where I got it. I got it through the mail, in an envelope, and that's all I'll tell you."

"It puts the bank in a very peculiar position," Canby said. "Of course, Mason, there is always a chance that the check that was drawn on *us* is a forgery."

"I thought you said your expert pronounced the signature genuine?"

"He has made a preliminary examination in which he says that there are indications the signature is genuine. In other words, there are no definite indications of forgery which he's been able to discover on that check, as yet."

"Well," Mason asked, "what are you trying to

do? Did you come to tell me that you weren't going to honor the check?"

"No, no, not at all."

"Well, what?"

"However," Canby said, "under the circumstances, I thought that you should know, and you might care to withdraw that check until such time as you can satisfy yourself."

"I'm satisfied now," Mason said. "The cashier says it's a good check. Your handwriting expert says it's a good check."

"But the check which was deposited with it was quite evidently a forgery, a very clever forgery."

"Well?"

"That, of course, would make the check drawn on us a subject for careful scrutiny."

"Hang it," Mason said, "*give* it careful scrutiny. That's what I've wanted all along. That's what I told you to do."

"I'd like to know something more about the circumstances under which those checks were received, Mr. Mason. And I hope you'll agree with me that the safe thing to do, under the circumstances, is to hold up payment until we can contact Mrs. Allred."

"Isn't the check good?"

"I don't know."

"Why not notify the police?"

"That, of course, might prove very embarrassing," Canby said, shifting his position uneasily. "The family is quite wealthy, Mr. Mason."

Mason said, "Look, you have a lawyer. I'm not

your lawyer. Why not ask him what to do about it. You're holding a check which may be forged. If it is forged, you want to apprehend the forger."

"Of course," Canby murmured, "our handwriting expert has been unable as yet to discover anything significant. It may take several days for him to get his records established. Even then he may run into some complicating circumstance. Generally, Mr. Mason, the bank is liable for payment of the forged check, whereas payment of a raised check depends on a question of negligence."

Mason grinned at him and said, "You'll pardon me, Canby. It's your baby."

"But it's *your* check — the one that's forged."

"So it is," Mason said.

"And we can't pass it for payment."

"That's your problem, Canby."

Gertie, the receptionist, appeared in the door with a telegram.

Mason nodded to Della Street. "See what it is, Della."

Della Street opened the telegram, looked at Mason rather quizzically, then glanced at Canby.

"Go ahead," Mason said. "Read it."

Della Street took it over and handed it to the lawyer.

Mason looked at it, said, "Humph," then read the wire aloud:

MAILED YOU CHECK FOR TWENTY-

41

FIVE HUNDRED DOLLARS PROTECT
MY DAUGHTER PATRICIA IN CASE
SHE NEEDS HELP BUT DON'T QUES-
TION HER ABOUT ANYTHING
LOLA FAXON ALLRED

"This wire," Mason said, "was sent from Springfield," and handed the message to the banker.

Canby studied it, said, "It's a day letter sent at nine o'clock this morning from Springfield. She refers to a twenty-five hundred dollar retainer, but, as I understand it, you received *two* twenty-five hundred dollar checks."

"That's right," Mason said. "One of them is apparently a forgery."

"Yes, yes, so it is."

"The other check apparently isn't. Mrs. Allred wants me to do something for her daughter. If you hold up payment on that check, it's your responsibility."

"Well," Canby said, "this wire is all our bank needs. The twenty-five hundred dollar check drawn on us will be put through to your account, Mr. Mason."

"I take it," Mason said quite casually, "there are ample funds in Mrs. Allred's account to cover the check."

The banker smiled. "Her account is *very* substantial, Mr. Mason."

"Just idle money?"

"She liked to have large cash balances, I believe."

42

"Do you know anything about this account at Las Olitas?"

"No, I don't."

"Well, thanks for calling," Mason said somewhat abruptly and Canby, recognizing that the interview was over, shook hands and departed, a quiet shadowy man, obviously dissatisfied with his interview.

As soon as the door closed, Mason said to Della Street, "That's a typical banker for you, Della. His handwriting expert can't find anything wrong with that first check, yet the bank is so cautious, it won't pay. Then along comes a telegram which has only a type written signature, but is on a sheet of perfectly genuine Western Union yellow paper, and the bank falls over itself being co-operative.

"Anyone can send a telegram he wants and sign any name to it he feels like — but bankers swallow anything which seems 'in due course' and choke to death over the unusual. The ideal way to approach a banker is with a rubber stamp.

"Go down the hall, Della; get Paul Drake of the Drake Detective Agency to come in here. I want to find out who actually sent the wire."

# Chapter 4

Paul Drake draped his loose-jointed length over the big client's chair, twisting around until he had a comfortable position. Then after a moment, he squirmed about until his legs were hanging over the overstuffed arm of the chair.

Paul Drake carefully cultivated a nondescript appearance and a lugubrious countenance. There was, to him, no romance in connection with the operation of a detective agency. He looked upon his profession with an air of pessimistic detachment, did his work competently and deprecatingly.

"Know anything about Bertrand C. Allred, Paul?" Mason asked.

"Very little. He's a big shot in the mining business. Wait a minute, I do know something too. I heard something just the other day. He's mixed up in a suit for fraud."

"His wife has skipped out," Mason said.

"Okay, where do I come in?"

Mason handed Paul Drake the telegram he had received, said, "I want to talk with Mrs. Allred. Here's a telegram that was sent earlier this morning from Springfield. I want you to find her."

"Got a description?" Drake asked.

Mason shook his head, said, "That's up to you, Paul. You'll have to work fast. She has a daughter,

Patricia Faxon, the one mentioned in the wire. Mrs. Allred's supposed to be running away with a man, Robert Fleetwood. That is highly confidential. The family doesn't want it to get out."

"When did she leave?"

"Saturday night on a guess. She sent me a check drawn on a local bank here for twenty-five hundred dollars. At any rate, the check seems to have been signed by her. That check was mailed Saturday night. This morning I received another check, drawn on the First National Bank of Las Olitas, also for twenty-five hundred dollars and also purporting to be signed by her."

"In the telegram," Drake pointed out, "she only refers to one check."

"That's right. One check of twenty-five hundred. That's the only one the bank says is good."

"What about the other one?"

"Handwriting experts say it's forged. The signature was transferred and re-traced."

"How about the checks, other than the signature?"

"In typewriting," Mason said. "Both checks are the same on that score, and the interesting thing is that as nearly as I can tell from an examination of the envelopes, they were both typed on the same typewriter."

"Okay," Drake said. "Give."

Mason gave him the two envelopes in which the checks had been received.

"Where are the checks?"

"One of them has been cleared," Mason said,

grinning, "and the other is in the hands of the bank. The bank may be contemplating turning it over to the police."

"The bank hasn't asked for the envelopes in which the checks came?"

"Not yet. It will. Have those envelopes photographed. Then have some enlargements made so we can check that typewriting. Get an expert to tell the make and model of typewriter on which they were written."

"That all?"

"That's all I can tell you. You'll probably think of something else as you go along."

Drake heaved himself up out of the chair. "How about this daughter, Patricia? Can I tell her about the wire?"

"I don't see why not."

"Tell her I'm from you?"

Mason thought for a moment, then said, "Tell her you're a newspaper reporter first. Let's see what story she has for publication. Then tell her who you are and say you're working for me. See if it changes her story."

"Anything else?" Drake asked.

Mason said, "I don't need to draw you a diagram, Paul. Police records are full of cases of wealthy wives who disappear, husbands who think up one story and then another. It all follows a pattern."

"You mean the husband bops the wife over the head, puts the body in the cellar, pours on a little cement, and then tells the neighbors his spouse has gone to visit 'Aunt Mary'?"

"That's the general idea."

"In this case there's a second person, Fleetwood."

"It may be a big cellar."

"Not let anyone know what's cooking, I suppose?"

"That's right."

"Shall I let Patricia know why you're looking for Mom?"

"No. Let her do the talking — and acting."

"Okay," Drake said. "How soon do you want this stuff?"

"Soon as I can get it," Mason said.

"You always do," Drake told him, and went out.

Mason said to Della Street, "You hold the fort, Della. I'm going to take a run out to Las Olitas. With luck I can see the bank president before he goes to lunch."

# Chapter 5

Las Olitas clung to the orchard covered foothills in drowsy contentment.

Here were the homes of ranchers who were making a good living from the country. Here also were the houses of wealthy people who had removed themselves from the hurry and the bustle of the city to the tranquillity of the rich little suburb.

Situated a thousand feet higher than the plain below, with a backdrop of rugged mountains behind it, Las Olitas was bathed in sunshine. From its residential section, one looked out over a bluish haze of atmospheric impurities to the place where the big city belched nauseous gases into the air.

It was a forty minute drive from Mason's office to the main street of Las Olitas, and Mason paused for a moment to admire the clear blue of the sky, the slopes of the mountains in the background. Then the lawyer left his car in a parking lot and walked a short distance to the First National Bank.

The institution seemed to reflect the temperament of the community. Large, spacious and carefully designed by skillful architects, the bank was permeated with an atmosphere of placid stability.

Mason, running his eyes down the row of open offices back of a marble partition, found a brass plaque bearing the words, *"C.E. Pawling, President."* Mason also noticed that Mr. Pawling was, for the moment, disengaged.

The lawyer moved over to the marble partition and studied the president, a man of around sixty who wore an expensively tailored suit with an air of distinction, whose keen, steady eyes managed to radiate a smiling welcome to the world at large, yet all the time those eyes were making a hard appraisal based on shrewd objective observation.

Mason bowed and the man behind the desk instantly arose and came over to the marble counter.

"My name is Mason," the lawyer said.

Pawling extended his hand.

"I'm a lawyer."

"Yes, Mr. . . . not *Perry* Mason?"

"Yes."

"Well, well, Mr. Mason! This is indeed a pleasure! Won't you come in? I've read a lot about you. Are you thinking of opening an account, Mr. Mason?"

"No," Mason said, as he walked through the mahogany gate which the bank president had opened. "I came to see you about a matter which, quite frankly, has puzzled me — the matter having to do with the interest and welfare of one of your depositors."

"Indeed, Mr. Mason. Do sit down. Tell me about it."

Mason said, "I received a check in the mail this morning, a check drawn on this bank in an amount of twenty-five hundred dollars."

"Ah, yes," Pawling said, his tone indicating that twenty-five hundred dollar retainers could well be paid by the majority of the depositors in his bank.

"I deposited that check with my own bank in the city, the Farmers, Merchants & Mechanics Bank."

Pawling nodded.

"You have perhaps heard about it?" Mason asked.

Pawling said suavely, "I'd have to learn more of the details, Mr. Mason."

"The person who signed that check," Mason said, "was Lola Faxon Allred. She has an account also at this same bank where I carry my account. In examining the signature on the check, the bank officials became suspicious, called in a handwriting expert, and the handwriting expert pronounced the check a forgery."

"Indeed."

"I suppose that you were notified."

"What is it you wish, Mr. Mason?"

Mason said, "I also received another check from Lola Faxon Allred, in an amount of twenty-five hundred dollars."

Pawling was sitting quite straight in his chair now, his head tilted slightly so that he would be sure to catch every word the lawyer said.

"That check," Mason said, "was good as gold.

It was sent to me by way of a retainer to represent Mrs. Allred in certain matters which concerned her. I am, therefore, in the position of having been a recipient of a forged check and the payee in a genuine check. I am also in the position of being Mrs. Allred's attorney."

"Ah, yes," Pawling said.

Mason said, "My client is not available at the moment."

"Indeed."

"It occurs to me that the check on this bank which I received may not have been the only forgery which was perpetrated. Mrs. Allred, I believe, customarily makes her checks on a typewriter, does she not?"

"I believe so. Yes."

"And only the signature in her handwriting?"

Pawling nodded.

Mason said, "I gather from certain things that I learned, that her account here is not too active. Of course, if a bank pays a forged check, the liability is that of the bank. But, I feel certain that my client would wish to take immediate steps to see that no further forgeries are perpetrated."

Pawling pressed a button on his desk.

A secretary appeared from an adjoining office, became instantly attentive.

Pawling said, "Will you please get me a statement of the account of Lola Faxon Allred and cover all of the windows. I want any checks that have been presented today on the account."

The secretary withdrew.

Mason said, "Am I correct in assuming the account is not very active?"

"I believe Mrs. Allred likes to have large amounts of cash on hand. She likes to keep her affairs in a rather liquid condition. I am assuming that as Mrs. Allred's lawyer, you will not ask for information which she would not care to have given to you."

"I feel certain that I will make no such request."

Pawling nodded.

The secretary returned carrying a letter and a canceled check.

"The cashier intended to call this matter to your attention at the bank meeting tomorrow. He thought perhaps you should know about it, although it seems to be entirely regular in form. You will notice that the letter is addressed to him."

Pawling took the letter and the canceled check, held both documents guardedly so that Mason could not see them. He studied the letter and the check for a few seconds, then drummed silently with the tips of his fingers on the edge of the desk.

At length he looked up and nodded to his secretary, said, "That's all."

The girl withdrew. Pawling turned to Mason. His eyes were no longer smiling. They were hard and steady in their appraisal.

"You have some reason for presenting this matter to me, Mr. Mason?"

"Well, yes."

"May I ask what it is?"

Mason said, "My client retained me to look after certain interests. Then she became unavailable. The circumstances surrounding her departure are not entirely routine. It occurred to me that perhaps someone, knowing of her intended departure, had taken deliberate advantage of it to start making withdrawals from her account."

"The forgery was done cleverly?"

"I believe so. Carbon paper and tracing, but it was detected by my bank, after I myself requested the officials of the bank to give the check the closest scrutiny."

"In other words, you had some reason to think that the check had been forged?"

"I had reason to believe it might be to the interests of my client to have the check given very close scrutiny."

"But, as I understand it, Mr. Mason, this check was purportedly for the purpose of retaining you to represent Mrs. Allred."

"The other check was for that purpose."

"But why should someone forge *any* check in *your* favor, Mr. Mason?"

The lawyer smiled. "That is one of the things I would like to determine."

Pawling studied the letter and check for a few moments, and then abruptly reached a decision and passed them both to Mason.

The lawyer read the letter which was addressed to the cashier of the First National Bank at Las Olitas. It was entirely in typewriting, except for the signature, and read:

This will introduce to you Maurine Milford, whose signature appears immediately above mine, on the left-hand edge of this letter.

I am today giving Maurine Milford my check for five thousand dollars and I wish this check to be paid upon presentation without asking Maurine Milford for any identification, other than that contained in this letter.

You will notice that the check is payable to Miss Milford, that she has endorsed the check and that I, in turn, have signed the check under her endorsement, guaranteeing her signature.

I am also giving you this letter, so that there can be no doubt of Miss Milford's identity. Please co-operate by seeing that this check is promptly cashed.

Very truly yours,
LOLA FAXON ALLRED

Over in the left-hand corner appeared the signature of Maurine Milford, and another signature of Lola Faxon Allred.

The check in an amount of five thousand dollars had been signed *Lola Faxon Allred*, then endorsed *Maurine Milford*, and under that endorsement appeared the signatures once more of Lola Faxon Allred and Maurine Milford.

"What do you make of it?" Pawling asked.

Mason gave the letter frowning consideration. "Do you have a magnifying glass there?" he asked.

"A very powerful one," Pawling said, and opened the drawer of his desk.

Mason studied the signatures, said, "I'm no handwriting expert, but I would say that these signatures have not been made by the same means as the forged signature on the twenty-five hundred dollar check."

Pawling nodded.

Mason went on, "The fact that Mrs. Allred went to such pains to see that Maurine Milford was provided with a means of identification is some indication that it might have been difficult for Miss Milford to have secured any other identification. In other words, Miss Milford is quite evidently a stranger here."

Again the banker contented himself with a mere nod.

"And, quite apparently, there was some necessity for haste in connection with the transaction," Mason said. "I see that the letter and the check were dated last Saturday. The documents were presented this morning."

Mason turned the letter over, noticed a rubber stamp announcing the hour of receipt by the bank and said, "Apparently it was presented a few minutes after ten o'clock. Perhaps it would be a good plan to find out whether the cashier knows Maurine Milford."

Pawling started to press the button, then

checked himself, picked up the letter and the check, said, "Excuse me a moment, Mr. Mason," and quietly opening the mahogany gate in his office walked unhurriedly along the long length of the corridor, to pause before the cashier's window.

When he returned, he was carrying a slip of paper on which he had apparently jotted down the description which the cashier had given him.

"Maurine Milford," the banker said, "is apparently a rather striking young woman, in the very early twenties, a decided brunette with dark eyes and long lashes. She was wearing a powder blue suit and dark blue suede gloves. She had a blue suede purse and an eccentric hat with red trim which perched on one side of her head. She took off her gloves when she presented the check. The cashier took the precaution of having her sign an additional endorsement, to show she had received the money, and then paid her the money in hundred dollar bills. The cashier remembers that she was well-formed, slim-waisted and athletic-looking. She seemed thoroughly at ease, perfectly in command of herself and the situation. She smilingly parried all questions as to what she intended to do with the money. It was, of course, none of the cashier's business, so he was tactful. He merely asked her whether she intended to establish a residence here, whether she would like to open an account, what denomination she would like the bills in, and things of that sort.

"The only thing which the cashier noticed that

was at all conspicuous about her, aside from the fact that she was quite beautiful, was that her make-up was quite heavy, particularly the lips. The lipstick seemed to be rather vivid and the natural shape of the mouth had been radically distorted and thickened. As soon as her check was paid, she put the money in her purse and walked out.

"And that, Mr. Mason, seems to be about all we know concerning the transaction. I shall, of course, have a handwriting expert immediately check this letter and the signature on the check, but you will note there are three signatures — one on the letter, one on the face of the check, one on the back of the check under the endorsement of Maurine Milford. Each one of those signatures seems to be entirely genuine."

The banker paused, inviting Mason's further confidence.

The lawyer pushed back his chair. "Will you," he asked, "telephone me at once, in the event there should be any question on the part of your handwriting expert?"

Pawling nodded.

Mason said, "I take it he will make a preliminary examination and then perhaps a more detailed examination. I should like to be kept advised."

"I feel certain you are entitled to that courtesy."

Mason, turning over the letter in his hand, said casually, "I'm not certain that you advised me as to whether there had been any other unusual

57

activity on the part of Mrs. Allred's account lately."

Pawling said, "This is the only withdrawal that has been made during a period — well, of some time, Mr. Mason."

Abruptly, Mason tilted the letter to one side so that light struck it from an angle. Then he slid the tips of his fingers over the signature.

"Something?" the banker asked.

Mason said, "I would say that we may now safely put two and two together. You'll notice a very slight indentation along the lines of this signature. Quite evidently, this was the signature from which the signature on the forged check was traced."

"Dear, dear!" Pawling said as though he had suffered some minor irritation such as breaking the point of a pencil.

Mason regarded him quizzically. "A matter of some twenty-five hundred dollars," he said.

Pawling positively beamed, "Which the bank has not paid, of course."

"That does not alter the seriousness of the crime," Mason said.

"No, I suppose not."

"Nor the fact that I feel something should be done about it."

"Such as what, Counselor?"

"Taking steps to see that no other forged checks are cashed."

"That, of course, will be done, almost as a routine — fancy a forged check being used to retain a lawyer to ask that the account be protected from further forgeries! One would almost think that . . ."

"Yes, go on," Mason said as the banker hesitated.

"That it had been planned that way."

"Well, it wasn't," Mason snapped.

"No, no, of course not! I merely said one would *almost* think so."

"Thank you," the lawyer said, "for stopping your thinking at the almost," and walked out.

Mason handed his oblong parking ticket to the attendant of the lot next to the bank, said, "Were you on duty at ten o'clock?"

The attendant nodded, said cautiously, "What's the trouble?"

"No trouble," Mason said. "I wanted to get some information about someone who parked an automobile here for a few minutes."

The man laughed and said, "Look, buddy, in order to keep this lot running, we have to handle hundreds of automobiles in the course of a day and . . ."

"This young woman," Mason interrupted, "is one you probably would have noticed. She had a good figure, a tight-fitting blue suit, blue suede purse, a saucy little hat with red trim, on one side of her head, long dark eyelashes . . ."

"Would I have noticed a number like that!" the man said with enthusiasm. "Just hearing you describe her makes my mouth water. What about her?"

"Nothing, if you didn't notice her."

"I don't think she parked her car here. You say it was this morning?"

"Almost exactly at ten o'clock this morning."

"I don't think so. We're not too busy at ten o'clock in the morning. It isn't until the streets begin to fill up that they start coming in here."

Mason thanked him, paid for his car, circled around the block and drove into the parking station across the street from the bank.

"You on duty at ten this morning?" he asked the attendant.

The man hesitated before answering.

Mason said, "You're eligible for a five dollar reward, if you were."

"That's different! What's the reward for?"

"I am trying to find out something about a girl about twenty, twenty-one, or twenty-two years old, blue suit, nice figure, brunette, blue leather purse, blue gloves, a tricky little hat on one side of her head, who . . ."

"What do you want to know about her?"

"Anything I can find out. Do you remember her?"

"I think I do. What about the five bucks?"

"A little information about the make and model of the car she was driving, or anything of that sort."

The man grinned. "Give me the five bucks, mister."

Mason passed him a five dollar bill.

"It's a Chrysler convertible from a drive-yourself agency in the city. I don't know the name of the agency, but I know it was a drive-yourself outfit. I remember her because she was a neat little number and I was especially nice to her. Sometimes that gets you something."

"Get you anything this time?" Mason asked.

"A smile."

"That's all?"

"That was enough."

"You didn't try to find out anything about her or . . ."

"Nope. She wasn't that kind."

"That's all you know?"

"That's it."

Mason said, "Play the ponies with the five bucks. Perhaps you'll be lucky."

"Perhaps I will. Thanks."

From a telephone Mason called Drake's office and when he had the detective on the line, said, "Paul, I want you to cover the drive-yourself agencies. I want you to find out anything you can about a woman around twenty-one, twenty-two, or twenty-three, who rented a drive-yourself car this morning." Swiftly he described her. "She may or may not have given the name of Milford. She had a Chrysler convertible, and I want every place in the city covered and covered fast."

"Okay," Drake said. "Anything else?"

"That's all. What's new at your end?"

Drake said, "I haven't made too much headway, Perry. I haven't been able to get a photograph of Mrs. Allred, as yet. Patricia Faxon left

61

the house shortly after nine o'clock this morning and hasn't been back since. No one seems to know exactly where she is. I've found the place where the runaway couple stayed in Springfield. Provided it *is* the runaway couple and not a couple of ringers who are acting as red herrings."

"How come?" Mason asked.

"This couple," Drake said, "showed up in a motel at Springfield a little after midnight Saturday. They wanted a double cabin. The motel had only one left. They took it. The woman was driving the car and she conducted all the negotiations and did the registering. The man sat in the car with his arms folded, apparently too lazy to move, and didn't show the slightest interest in what was going on. The woman registered as 'R.G. Fleetwood and Sister,' and said they would occupy the cabin for two nights.

"Sunday morning, the woman went over to the motel office and inquired about renting dishes and about a grocery store that would be open on Sunday."

"Was there a kitchen in the double cabin they occupied?" Mason asked.

"That's right. The motel rented her a set of dishes and told her where she could buy groceries. She drove off and returned with a big basket of groceries on the seat beside her."

"Did the man go with her?"

"No. She said he was sleeping, he liked to sleep late on Sunday mornings. The woman evidently did all the cooking all day Sunday, and also this morning. She showed up about nine-thirty this morning, returning the dishes all nicely cleaned and polished, announced that they were checking out, and left shortly after. No one seems to know in which direction she was headed."

"They got in about midnight Saturday?" Mason asked.

"That's right. It may have been a half an hour after midnight, but I figure a good two hours' driving time from here to Springfield, so they must have left around — oh, say around ten o'clock in the evening, and figuring that they might have got into Springfield at half an hour or so after midnight, you can figure they must have left the city by ten-thirty at the latest."

"And the woman wanted a *double* cabin?"

"That's right, insisting that it must have three separate beds."

"Why did she want three separate beds for herself and her brother?"

"She didn't say. Simply said she wanted a double cabin. She preferred one double bed and twin beds. Of course, at the time, the people at the motel didn't ask how many were in the party. They acted on the assumption there would be three, at least, and fixed the price accordingly."

"How about descriptions?" Mason asked.

"Descriptions check as nearly as I can get them," Drake said. "Of course, the woman could have been a ringer and it could all be a beautiful red herring. I also have something on the telegram. The telegram was sent from Springfield by a woman who telephoned in from a pay station. She was advised that the charge for the telegram would be forty cents, and dropped the forty cents into the coin slot of the pay station telephone. That's all Western Union knows about it."

Mason laughed and said, "The bank unhesitatingly accepts the telegram as confirming the check and it now appears the telegram has no greater authenticity than a voice saying it belonged to Lola Faxon Allred."

"That's right," Drake said. "I couldn't get anything more on the man. The only time anyone saw him was in the car when they arrived."

"That's a hell of a way for a man who's running away with a married woman to act," Mason said. "He didn't show any interest in the accommodations?"

"No, while the woman made all the arrangements, he just sat there, slumped down in the seat."

Mason said, "All right. Keep plugging on this car rental business. I want to get this girl located. I have a hunch the car was rented this morning, probably around nine o'clock, and there's just a chance it hasn't been turned in yet. Sprinkle enough operatives around so that when she returns the car, you can put a shadow on her."

"Okay, Perry. I'll get some men on the job."

"And start covering hotels, tourist camps, motels and all the rest of it to try and find a trace of this couple," Mason said.

Drake said irritably, "What the hell do you

64

think we're doing, Perry?"

"Probably thinking up some new way to pad expense accounts," Mason said, and hung up.

# Chapter 6

It was three-thirty when Mason's unlisted telephone rang sharply. This unlisted telephone was on Mason's desk. Only Della Street and Paul Drake held that number, and the lawyer, scooping up the telephone, said, "Yes, Paul. What is it?"

Drake's voice, sharp with urgency, said, "We've located the girl who rented the car from the drive-yourself agency, Perry!"

"Great stuff!" Mason said. "What about her?"

"She took it out about nine o'clock this morning, giving the name of Jane Smith, and a phony address in Denver," Drake said. "She put up a large cash deposit and said she'd return the car about two this afternoon. We had that much uncovered about an hour after my men started work. I didn't notify you because there wasn't anything particular to go on at that time. I simply put operatives around to tail her when she drove back."

"Go ahead," Mason said.

"She came back a little over an hour ago," Drake said, "and wanted to make a deal by which she could rent a car by the week. She said she was going to be living in one of the suburbs, and there wouldn't be any great amount of mileage run up on the car, that she wanted to use it just for running back and forth. The drive-yourself agency worked out the deal with her and, of course, my men picked up her trail as soon as she left."

"Did she have any idea she was being tailed?"

"I don't think so."

"Where did she go?"

"I don't know yet, Perry. My men are shadowing her. I've got a couple of damn good men on the job and they'll run her to earth. I just wanted to be sure you'd be standing by."

"The same woman?"

"No question about it. The description fits to a *T*. It's the only Chrysler that's been rented to a woman who comes anywhere near answering your description. It looks like pay dirt to me."

"It does to me too," Mason said.

"Okay, I'll have something most any minute now."

The lawyer hung up and Della Street said, "Gertie says George Jerome is in the office waiting."

"Jerome?" Mason asked, frowning.

"Mr. Allred's partner in some mining deals. He wants to see you, but won't say what it's about. He says it's highly confidential."

Mason said, "All right. Hold everything open for that call that's coming in from Paul Drake. As soon as we get that woman in the Chrysler located, I want to get in touch with her. Send Jerome in."

Della Street went out to the reception room to usher Jerome into Mason's private office.

George Jerome was plainly impatient, a man who was not accustomed to waiting anywhere for anyone. He was tall, barrel-chested, rawboned with high cheek bones and from under shaggy brown eyes looked out upon the world in cold appraisal.

He was perhaps fifty-five or sixty, and the man radiated awkward strength as he lumbered across the office to shake hands with Mason.

"Sit down," the lawyer invited. "I've been wanting to see you."

"What about?"

Mason smiled. "About the thing you want to see me about."

Jerome returned the lawyer's smile. "If you're a mind reader, then there's no point of my saying anything."

Jerome settled himself in the big client's chair and the size of the man made the chair shrink in proportion until it seemed to lose its atmosphere of deep comfort.

"What's Allred up to?" he asked.

"I'm afraid I can't help you on that," Mason said.

"Are you Allred's lawyer?"

"No."

"Whose?"

Mason said, "At this time I feel there is no need to make further concealment of the name of my client. I am Mrs. Allred's attorney."

"Have you actually seen Lola Allred?"

"Why?"

"I just wanted to know."

"You've talked with Allred?" Mason asked.

"I've listened to him."

"You're his partner?"

"In a way, yes. That is, I'm his partner in some things. We're in process of settling up our affairs. We were supposed to have settled them Saturday. He was to have made a take-it-or-leave-it proposition. I didn't want to act until after I'd talked with Fleetwood."

"May I ask why?"

"He's a bright boy. He's been Allred's right-hand man — but if I bought Allred out, I think Bob Fleetwood would come over to work with me. I think he would. I'd want to make certain."

"Is he that valuable?"

"He knows lots of details no one else does."

"Then your intention is to buy Allred out?"

"I didn't say that."

"You implied it."

"I might imply lots of things. Have you talked with Lola Allred personally?"

"Why do you keep coming back to that question?"

"Because you keep avoiding it."

Mason laughed.

Jerome said, "You're a deep one, Mason."

The lawyer shook his head. "Flattery won't get you anywhere, Jerome."

"What will?"

"Candor."

Jerome said, "All right, I'll try that. I want you to get hold of Fleetwood. I want to have a secret conference with him. I want to see whether he will come over to me, pull with me, play the game my way. When I go into a business deal, I try to drive the best bargain I can. But when I make a deal, I stand by it. I'm not like Allred. He's always squirming around. You make an agreement with him and he remembers it some other way, and he never will put anything in writing. He always says that's up to his lawyer and his lawyer stalls along just as much as he does.

"Bob Fleetwood is a good kid. Allred says Bob ran away with his wife. If you ask me, I think it was something that was wished off on Bob. I think that Mrs. Allred may have gone for him pretty strong and, the first thing the kid knew, he was being taken for a ride. I'm not saying so, you understand, but that's *one* explanation."

"Is there another?"

"Yes."

"What?"

"The other explanation is that Mrs. Allred isn't alive at all, and Bert is trying to account for her disappearance. You're a lawyer. I don't need to dot the *i*'s or cross the *t*'s for you, Mason. I'm giving you an idea."

"And in that event, where would Fleetwood be?"

"Now then," Jerome said, "you're beginning to talk the way I want to hear you talk."

"Yes?" Mason asked.

Jerome said, "I'm making you a proposition, Mason. If you can get me a chance to talk with Bob Fleetwood before Allred sees him, I'll pay you a thousand dollars. And if Fleetwood sees things my way, and I'm satisfied he will, you get two thousand dollars. You hire detectives if you have to. I'll stand their charges, anything up to a thousand dollars."

"That's all right," Mason said, "but I can't accept any employment from you which might be adverse to the best interests of my client."

"I know you can't. I know your reputation, Mason. You're just as clean as a hound's tooth and as smart as a steel trap. That's why I came to you. Forget it, *unless it turns out that you can do it without interfering with the interests of your client.* You're representing Mrs. Allred. You go ahead and represent her, but if you find that you can give me a break on this thing, you've had my proposition.

"If you're Mrs. Allred's attorney, she's going to get in touch with you sooner or later. If Bob Fleetwood is running away with her, you'll have a chance to get word to him through her, or directly to him, that I've got to see him. That's all there is to it. And if Lola Allred *isn't* alive, then you're going to find that out, and when you do, you may find Fleetwood. The proposition stands win, lose or draw."

"What makes you think that Mrs. Allred may not be alive?"

Jerome looked steadily at Mason, then he closed one eye in a slow, calculating wink.

He got up from the chair, said, "I think I've made my proposition plain, Mr. Mason."

He turned to Della Street. "You've got all this straight, young lady?"

She nodded.

"Good. How do I get out of here?"

Mason indicated the exit door.

Jerome said, "Here's my card, Mason. There's a number on there you can call. I'll have someone at that phone day and night, twenty-four hours a day. The minute you call that number, you're in touch with me. And you can tell Fleetwood that well, dammit, tell him what I want. Fleetwood knows me and he knows Allred. Thank you, Mr. Mason. Good day."

And Jerome strode out of the office without bothering to shake hands or to even look back over his shoulder.

Mason turned to Della Street, but before he spoke the unlisted phone rang sharply.

Della Street picked up the receiver, said, "Hello . . . yes, hold the line, Paul."

Mason grabbed the phone.

"Just had a report from my men who trailed this auto-rental girl, Perry."

"Good! What happened?"

"She went directly to Las Olitas, stopped in at a garage there, the Central Garage & Machine Works on Eighth Street, was in there about five minutes, then she came out and drove to the

Westwick. That's an exclusive apartment hotel."

"Calling on someone there?" Mason asked.

"She lives there, Perry."

"The devil she does!"

"That's right."

"What name? Jane Smith?"

"No, Maurine Milford. She rented apartment
802 there recently, and she's expecting her aunt
to come from the East and join her. Tells a perfectly straightforward story. She put the rented
car in the garage at the Westwick and tipped the
attendant at the apartment garage five bucks, and
told him her aunt was coming to visit her, that
she was going to be doing quite a bit of running
around, that she had rented this car, that she'd
like to have it kept dusted off and the windshield
cleaned."

"How long does she intend to be there?"

"She told the management about thirty
days."

"Why did she stop at the Central Garage &
Machine Works, Paul?"

"I don't know. Probably some minor trouble
with the car, a spark plug or something. My man
didn't try to go in there and find out. He just
stuck around the entrance and waited for her to
come out; then he followed her to the Westwick."

"Okay," Mason said. "That's fine. What else
is new? Anything?"

"Nope. Still working on the runaway couple,"
Drake said. "Here's a funny one, Perry. There's

another detective agency on the job."

"You sure?"

"Yes."

"Who's hired them?"

"I don't know, but there are private detectives combing the country. Somehow I have an idea they're after the man instead of the woman."

"You mean Fleetwood?"

"That's right."

"Any idea why?"

"Only that they've been paid by someone to get information on him. When they ask questions, they ask about Fleetwood first and describe the man before they describe the woman."

"What's Fleetwood's description?" Mason asked.

"Around five foot seven or seven and a half. Weight about a hundred and thirty-five pounds. Dark eyes, wavy hair, rather romantic looking."

"No wonder Mrs. Allred is supposed to have gone overboard for him," Mason said.

"That's the way it looks," Drake said, "but this Mrs. Allred is quite a dish herself. She may be forty-two, but from all the dope I can get, she looks around thirty."

"Any pictures yet?"

"I've got one of her in a bathing suit that isn't too good as far as the face is concerned, but it's swell for the figure. And believe me, she's got one!"

"Have you been able to find Patricia yet?"

"No. She dusted out shortly after breakfast and

hasn't been back since."

"Okay," Mason said, "keep plugging. I'll go see this Milford gal. Keep your man on the job until I get there, then he can go."

# Chapter 7

Mason circled the block which contained the Westwick Apartment Hotel, a twelve-story, commodious building with wide, individual balconies and sun porches for the front apartments, a modern building streamlined in appearance and thoroughly in keeping with the quiet, aristocratic atmosphere of Las Olitas.

Mason kept on driving, his forehead creased in thought. He turned down Eighth Street, found the Central Garage & Machine Works and went in.

It was a big garage with more than a dozen mechanics working in busy efficiency.

A workman was buffing a fender with a portable wheel from which sparks were fanning out in a stream. Over in a corner a man with a paint gun was spraying a fog of paint over the side of a car. The sound of hammers kept up an intermittent tattoo.

Mason found the manager, said, "I'm trying to find a witness."

"Lots of people are. Mean anything for me?"

"It might."

"What's the name?"

"Jane Smith mean anything to you?"

"I'd have to look in the books. I don't recall a Jane Smith offhand."

"Doing anything right now for a Jane Smith?"

"I don't think so."

"She was in here this morning."

"I don't place her."

"How about a Maurine Milford?"

"That's different."

"Has she got a car here?"

"She's a customer. I can't tell you anything about her."

"Not her address?"

"Not her address."

"Could I look at the car?" Mason asked.

"Got anything for *me* to look at?"

"I could show you an engraving."

"Of what?"

"One of our past presidents."

"I like engravings. I used to collect them."

Mason took a bill from his wallet. The manager looked at it with calm appraisal.

Mason took another one from his billfold, placed it on top of the first, extended them both to the manager. "Rather nice work," he said.

"Yours?" the garage man asked.

"Have a little engraving press," Mason said. "I'm a great admirer of art, and I'm particularly fond of reproducing engravings of our former presidents."

"That's fine. Want to take a look at this car?"

Mason followed the garage man back through a door into another part of the shop. The manager motioned toward a new Lincoln.

"This it?" Mason asked.

"This is it."

"What's wrong with it?"

"Not much, now. There was a broken headlight, a bent fender and a few scratches."

"She run into something?"

"Naw. Her child is a precocious little youngster and ran plumb out of teething rings. She left him sitting in the car while she went in to see the doc about changing his food formula. When she got back the little chap had squirmed out of the car and chewed the hell out of the fender, then he bent it trying to get up and smash the headlight in."

"And this is Maurine Milford's car?"

"I didn't say that."

"I thought you did."

"The car," the garage man went on, "belongs to a friend of hers. She had it out driving when the accident happened. She wants to have it all fixed up so that her friend won't know it's been in an accident. That's why it's a rush job. It'll be ready to roll out tonight, and the owner won't be able to tell it even had a scratch."

"Who's the owner?"

"Me," the garage man said, "I'm just dumb. You're looking over the car. Seems to me it has a license on it, and there's a state law, as I remember it, that says you have to have a certificate of registration attached to the steering post. Personally, I wouldn't know anything about that. I'm going back to the shop now. I got some work to do. What did you say your name was?"

"I didn't say," Mason told him. "I'm just an engraver."

"Well, I always like to talk to a man who goes in for that sort of art. Any time you have more pretty pictures, bring 'em around."

Mason watched him leave the room; then the lawyer opened the door of the car, climbed into the driver's seat, found the registration certificate attached to the steering post. The car was registered in the name of Patricia Faxon. The address was 209 West Mayward Avenue.

The lawyer sat there for a few moments. Then he slid out of the car and walked out of the garage. He drove directly to the Westwick Apartments.

Mason didn't announce himself, but took the elevator to the eighth floor, found apartment 802, and pressed the button.

A young, vivacious girl, in a neatly tailored blue suit opened the door and regarded him with laughing, dark eyes.

But the lips were not garishly painted. They were almost subdued so that the eyes dominated the face.

"You're Miss Milford," he said.

"That's right."

"I'd like to talk to you."

She laughed and said, "I have all the insurance I want, the apartment is furnished, I have plenty of books, and I don't need a thing. I am not going to be here long enough to buy a radio. I don't need a vacuum cleaner because that goes with the apartment maid service and . . ."

"I'm John Smith," Mason said.

"Are you, indeed!"

"Yes," he said. "Jane Smith's older brother."

"Oh," she said, and then suddenly the animation left her face. She was showing him a mask of cautious appraisal. "Jane Smith. I don't think I know her."

"She rented a car from a drive-yourself agency," Mason said. "She was last seen headed in the direction of Las Olitas."

"Come in," the girl invited.

Mason entered the living room of the apartment suite.

"I understand," he said, "you are expecting your aunt to join you."

"Yes."

"And why the Jane Smith part of it when you rented the car?"

She said, "For reasons that I can't explain I didn't want to tell the car agency what my real name was or where I intended to live. I suppose I've violated some rule or regulation, and if you'll tell me how much it is, I'll give you the money and we'll get all square."

"It isn't a matter of money," Mason said, "but we like to know something about the moral risk involved, particularly when a car goes out for a long time."

"All right. You can find out all you want about the moral risk. You have the cash deposit which certainly is generous enough to protect you. If you want, I'll double that deposit or treble it."

Mason said, "Money doesn't take the place of a good moral risk."

She laughed up at him and said, "Go on! Money beats morals any time. Just *what* are you after?"

"I'd like a case history."

"Well, begin at the beginning. Just what do you want to know?"

"In the first place, why do you want an automobile?"

"I told your people. My aunt is coming to visit me. She's never been in California before, and I want to show her around. Then again, I like to have an automobile for my own convenience."

"You're from the East?"

"I didn't say that."

"Can you tell me where you were living before you came here?"

"I can, but I won't."

"You have driven an automobile before?"

"Naturally."

"You have a driving license?"

"No."

Mason said, "Under the clause in the insurance policy, the company is supposed to let out automobiles only to persons who hold a driving license."

"I do."

"I'd like to look at it."

"I gathered that, but I see no reason to show it to you."

"Have you," Mason asked, "had any trouble with driving an automobile? Have you been in

81

any accidents within the past sixty days?"

"No."

"Then," Mason asked, "how does it happen that you are having the car of Miss Patricia Faxon repaired down here at the Central Garage & Machine Works?"

Her face went dead white at that. She looked at him for a long moment.

"Well?" Mason asked.

"Who are you?" she asked.

Mason said, "I'll put it up to you. Who are *you?*"

"I've told you I'm Maurine Milford."

Mason said, "I'm sorry, but I *think* you're Patricia Faxon, and the aunt who is planning to come and visit you for a month is your mother, Lola Faxon Allred. My name is Perry Mason, and now if you'll quit beating around the bush and tell me what it is you and your mother want, I may be able to help you."

There was the panic of sheer desperation in her eyes. "You . . . you're . . . you're Perry Mason!"

"That's right."

"How did you find me?"

"I simply traced you here."

"But you couldn't have. It's impossible. I've taken the greatest precautions. I've — why every time I've left the house, I've made absolutely certain I wasn't being followed. I've gone to the greatest pains to see that I didn't leave any back track and —"

Mason interrupted. "You left a back trail. I

followed it. My detectives followed it. The police can follow it."

"You weren't supposed to get in touch with me," she said. "I was supposed to get in touch with you."

Mason said, "If I'd known you were Patricia Faxon when I started, I might have made different plans, but unfortunately you neglected to tell me that you intended to take an assumed name and an assumed identity. Now suppose you tell me why?"

"Suppose I don't?"

Mason shrugged his shoulders. "It's up to you."

"I see no reason why I should, Mr. Mason. I'm going to tell you frankly that if — well, if certain things happen I'll get in touch with you, and if they don't, I won't, and that's final."

Mason said, "I received a check in the mail for twenty-five hundred dollars, signed by Lola Faxon Allred."

"I know you did."

"And," Mason went on, "you went to the bank at Las Olitas and drew out five thousand dollars, also on a check signed by Lola Faxon Allred."

"Well?"

Mason said, "The check I received was a forgery."

Her eyes widened. "A *forgery*, Mr. Mason?"

"That's right."

"It couldn't have been. I know all about that check. Mother signed it. I saw her sign it."

"A check on the First National Bank at Las Olitas?"

"No. On the Farmers, Merchants & Mechanics Bank in the city."

Mason said, "That was the other check."

"You mean you got *two* checks, Mr. Mason?"

"That's right."

"*Two* checks *each* for twenty-five hundred dollars?"

"Yes."

"But that's impossible!"

"I told you one of them was forged."

"Won't you — won't you please sit down, Mr. Mason?"

Mason settled himself comfortably in one of the big overstuffed chairs. "Nice place you have here," he said politely.

"Yes, I was very fortunate. What about this forged check?"

"All I can tell you is that the genuine signature from which the tracing was made was the signature on the letter your mother gave you for the cashier of the First National Bank here."

"The letter *I* had?" she asked incredulously.

"That's right, the Maurine Milford letter."

"Why, I — I don't believe it."

"And," Mason went on, "since your mother has eloped with your boy friend I thought that perhaps . . ."

"I beg your pardon, Mr. Mason! What are you talking about?"

"Your mother running off with your boy friend."

"Are you completely crazy, or are you laying some sort of a trap for me?"

"*Didn't* your mother run off with Robert Gregg Fleetwood?"

"What do you mean 'run off' with him?"

"Leave her husband and elope. Aren't they running away together and . . . ?"

"Certainly not!" she blazed. "What are you trying to do? Are you just trying to get a rise out of me?"

Mason said, "I'm trying to represent your mother, Patricia, and I'm supposed to represent you in case you get in a jam. If your mother hasn't gone off with Fleetwood, you'd better give me the facts, and fast."

"But the check, Mr. Mason. I don't see how in the world anyone could have . . ."

"Never mind the check for a minute," Mason said. "Let's get the lowdown on what's happened to Fleetwood."

"What do you mean 'what's happened to him'?"

Mason met her eyes steadily. "Did you," he asked, "strike him with your car, Patricia?"

For a moment her eyes met his, defiantly. Then under the steady gaze of the lawyer's eyes, her own eyes faltered.

"Did you?" Mason asked.

"Yes," she said.

"And that's why you're having your car repaired? Why you've created the identity of Maurine Milford — trying to conceal the evidence that would indicate you had struck someone with the left front fender of your automobile?"

She said, "It's a long story, Mr. Mason."

"Then the sooner you start on it, the quicker we'll get to an understanding."

"Have you ever been out to our house?" she asked.

Mason shook his head.

"It's virtually a double house," she said, "with a patio. As a matter of fact, there really are two houses. Mr. Allred uses the south wing for his offices. The north wing contains the living quarters, and between the two, and connecting them, are the garages with servants' quarters. It's just as though you had two houses separated by a vacant lot, with the garages running along the back of the vacant lot, and the vacant lot being used as a patio."

"Rather a public patio, isn't it?" Mason asked.

"That's the point. When Mr. Allred bought the place, he planted a hedge along the sidewalk. That hedge had now grown up very thick and heavy. It shuts the place off completely except for the gap where the driveway to the garages goes along the side of the north wing."

"And what does all this have to do with what happened to Robert Fleetwood?"

"I'm coming to that. The hedge is close to the driveway. In the course of time, as the hedge grew and expanded, despite all the trimming it's had, it's spread out into the driveway so that there's barely room to get a car through."

"That's all you want, isn't it?"

"Yes, but . . . you remember it was raining Saturday night?"

Mason nodded.

She said, "My mother and I had been to a cocktail party. I don't want you to think that we were the least bit tight, because we weren't. But we *had* had three or four cocktails apiece."

"Who was driving the car?"

"I was."

"And you hit Fleetwood?"

"Not exactly . . . well, it wasn't just like that."

"How was it?"

"When we started for home it was rather late, and I was making time. It had been raining heavily and visibility was poor. The wet pavement seemed to sop up the headlights. When we got home I swung around the corner and started to turn into the driveway. Then I noticed that Mr. Allred's car had been parked at the curb in such a way that the hind bumper actually stuck out just a little bit over the driveway. I probably could have stopped my car, backed around, made a perfectly straight run down the driveway and got into the garage. But as it was, I simply clipped a corner of the hedge. Well, the hedge was a little bigger and a little stronger than I had remembered it. The last time I put a car through the corner of the hedge it went through all right, but this time it — it struck something."

"Fleetwood?" Mason asked.

"At the time I thought it was merely a heavy branch."

"Is Fleetwood dead?"

"No, no. Don't misunderstand me. He sustained a head injury and he's suffering from amnesia. He can't remember a thing."

"And aside from that?"

"Aside from that, he's all right."

"When did you know you'd struck Fleetwood?"

"That's just the point, Mr. Mason. I didn't know it at the time. That's the unfortunate part of it. That's where all the trouble will come in."

"Go ahead."

"I knew that I'd struck something fairly solid, and said to Mother that that hedge certainly had grown up and that I guessed I'd nicked a bumper — and we both laughed. It seemed funny at the time. We were feeling good."

"Then what?"

"Then we drove into the one of the garages that's kept for my car, dashed into the house, showered and dressed for dinner.

"Mr. Allred told us that he and Bob Fleetwood had been working until late and he'd asked Bob to stay for dinner but Bob said he wanted to run down to his apartment and freshen up a bit first, that it would only take him fifteen or twenty minutes."

"Fleetwood's apartment is near your house?"

"That's right. Within two or three blocks. You see, he works with Mr. Allred at all hours of the day and night, so he got an apartment near by."

"Is he a special friend of yours?" Mason asked.

"Definitely not."

"Wants to be?"

"I think so, yes. In a wolfish sort of way."

"And doesn't get anywhere?"

"No."

"Then you haven't been crying your eyes out?"

"Over what?"

"Over what happened."

"I've been terribly upset over — well, over hitting him."

"You did hit him when you clipped the corner of the hedge?"

"Yes."

"When did you find it out?"

"Not until after dinner. We waited for Bob for nearly half an hour, then Mother decided to go ahead and have dinner. It was sometime during dinner that we mentioned to Mr. Allred that the hedge would have to be cut back and told him what had happened. He was full of apologies. He said he'd parked his car at the curb, intending to leave it there only for a few minutes. He hadn't realized that the car was in the way. He said he'd move it right away.

"It was still drizzling and dark. Mr. Allred went out to move his car away from the driveway, and

89

then — just as he backed it around to come down the driveway the headlights showed this — this object."

"Fleetwood?"

"Yes."

"You say he wasn't killed?"

"No, he was unconscious. Mr. Allred thought he was dead, but I'd had some first aid experience and I was able to find a pulse."

"So then what happened?"

"We brought him into the house. I started to telephone for a doctor, but Mr. Allred said we could put him in his car and he could get him to a hospital a lot quicker than we could wait for a doctor or an ambulance.

"Bob regained consciousness while we were talking. He opened his eyes and muttered something that was unintelligible, then closed his eyes again and then after a moment wanted to know where he was and wanted to know *who* he was.

"Of course, at the time, we felt that it was merely the fact that he was dazed. Apparently he'd struck his head on a curb when . . . when my fender had hit him."

"There's a walk on the inside of the hedge by the patio?" Mason asked.

"That's right. There's the public sidewalk along the street on the outside of the hedge, and then there's a walk along the inside, flagstones set into the lawn, but there's a cement curb, a sort of retaining wall running along the edge of the flagstone walk, with the lawn about eighteen inches higher than the flag walk."

"All right," Mason said. "Go on. What happened?"

"Well, it was obvious that the injury to Bob's head had given him amnesia. He didn't know who he was or where he was, or what it was all about."

"And then what happened?"

She said, "I don't know all of the details. I know that Mr. Allred and Mother had a whispered consultation and then went in the other room and talked for a while. You see, Bob Fleetwood is Mr. Allred's right-hand man. He knows a lot about the business, and right at the present time there are some very important matters pending."

"Such as what?" Mason asked.

"Well, for one thing, Mr. Jerome and Mr. Allred are having some trouble. I think they're ready to dissolve the partnership. It's a question of who pays the money and how much is taken. I think Fleetwood knows something there.

"Then there's the lawsuit with Dixon Keith. I think Fleetwood is the key witness there, and if people should know that Fleetwood had lost his memory — well, even if he got it back, you know what a lawyer would do. He'd get Bob on the stand and ask him if such and such wasn't the case, and if Fleetwood said 'No,' he'd ask him if it wasn't true he'd lost his memory for a while and ask him how he knew he had made a complete recovery. He'd make things pretty tough for Bob."

"So what?"

"So Mr. Allred decided that my mother had better tell Fleetwood she was his married sister, that Bertrand Allred was his brother-in-law, and I was his niece.

"And that's absolutely everything there was to it, Mr. Mason. My mother and my stepfather took Bob Fleetwood . . ."

"Wait a minute," Mason interrupted. "You mean your stepfather went with them?"

"Of course."

"Where did they go?"

"They intended to go to some outlying suburb where no one would ever think to look for Bob. They intended to register somewhere and keep him very, very quiet. They knew that's what a doctor would prescribe, to keep him quiet so as to avoid the aftereffects of concussion."

"You don't know where they went?"

"No."

"You do know that Bertrand Allred went with them?" Mason asked.

"Yes."

Mason got up from the chair and began pacing the floor, hands pushed down deep in his pockets, his head thrust slightly forward.

"What is it, Mr. Mason?" she asked.

Mason said, "Then your mother didn't have any romantic attachment for Fleetwood whatever?"

"Of course not. Certainly not."

"She simply took him to some motel or auto camp where he could be quiet for a while?"

"Yes."

"And Bertrand Allred knew about it?"

"He's the one who suggested it. He went with them."

Mason shook his head and said, "It doesn't make sense. Wait a minute. Yes, it does, too."

"What do you mean?"

Mason looked at his watch and said, "Where's your mother now?"

"I don't know."

"Any way of finding out?"

"She was going to communicate with me."

"What," Mason asked, "is the idea of all this buildup?" and he included the apartment with a gesture of his hand.

She said, "I feel like a heel about this, Mr. Mason, but it was Mother's idea. She thought that if — well, if anything happened and there *should* be any complications —"

"Go ahead."

"She thought that — well, in case anything happened, that it would be a lot better if I could adopt the position that I'd loaned the car on Saturday evening to some friend. So we created the identity of Maurine Milford and decided to build her up a bit. We decided to let her live here in Las Olitas, take Patricia Faxon's automobile in to have it repaired, tell a story about having hit something, try to keep the whole thing secret and . . ."

93

"And then as soon as any investigator started checking on the thing, he'd find that your description agreed with that of Patricia Faxon and would have discovered the whole scheme without any difficulty."

"It wasn't going to be that simple, Mr. Mason. I didn't think people would identify me. But they were never going to have a chance to do it, except from a general description. Whenever I've been out as Maurine Milford, I've had a special make-up on that changed the shape of my mouth and everything. A superficial description would have been the same, but — well, I don't think they could have proven anything. Within reasonable limits, we gals all look alike nowadays, except for details."

"Reasonable limits is right," Mason said.

"I know I shouldn't have done it."

"It was a damn fool thing to have done," Mason said.

"But at the time we didn't know — well, we didn't know whether it would turn out Bob was seriously injured. Of course, if he had been, Mother was going to call a doctor, but the way things were, Mr. Allred thought it would be better for them to simply — well, to go to some motel where they could be quiet and pretend they were traveling places."

"And where was Allred all this time?"

"Right there with them in the motel."

"You're sure?"

"Of course, I'm sure."

"Allred spent that night with your mother and Bob Fleetwood?"

"That's my understanding."

"And last night?"

She nodded.

"Where is he today?"

"Back at his office carrying on his business. He doesn't want anyone to suspect that Fleetwood isn't . . ."

Mason said, "Pat, I think it's up to you and me to find your mother without any delay."

"Why?"

"Because it was Bertrand Allred who told me your mother was eloping with Bob Fleetwood."

She thought that over for a space of almost a minute, then went to the coat closet, got her hat and coat and said, "Do you want me to go with you?"

"After a little while," Mason said. "There's no use rushing our heads off right now. I have a force of detectives combing every auto camp and motel looking for them."

"You think Mother is in some danger?"

"I'll put it this way. I don't think it was your car that hit Bob Fleetwood. I think things were fixed so it would be easy for you to clip the corner of the hedge. I think that the person who really hit Fleetwood thought he was dead and left the body where you'd get the blame. Now add to that the fact that Bertrand told me your mother had eloped with Fleetwood. Do you get the picture?"

She watched him with wide, startled eyes. "Do

you mean . . . what I think you mean?"

Mason nodded.

She said, "I saw him taking a revolver out of his desk drawer. Mr. Mason, we must *do* something."

The lawyer nodded, said, "Sit down, Patricia. We're doing it."

"You mean there's nothing to do except wait?"

"That's right. I have men covering the country."

She sat down. "I can't believe Bertrand Allred would . . . would do a thing like that."

"So far it's just a guess on my part," Mason said.

"No, no. It's the truth. A dozen things point to it. I can see it all now."

Mason said, "Here's my telephone number at my apartment. Get your car. Go back to your home. Keep an eye on Mr. Allred. Keep the porch light on. If he starts to take his car out of the garage, switch the porch light off. That's all you have to do. I'll have detectives take over from there."

# Chapter 8

It was seven-thirty in the evening when the unlisted telephone in Mason's apartment began ringing.

The lawyer, who had been studying the Advance Decisions, closed the printed pamphlet and picked up the telephone.

Patricia Faxon's voice was sharp with panic. "I've failed, Mr. Mason," she said.

"In what?"

"Mr. Allred managed to slip one over on me, somehow."

"What do you mean?"

"He's gone. He isn't here. I'm alone in the house. But he hasn't taken his automobile out of the garage. It's still there. I don't know how he could have left."

"Were there any visitors at the house?" Mason asked.

"Yes. That is, not right at the house. I think I told you he has an office in the south wing. He was over there during the first part of the evening, and he had at least one visitor."

"Know who it was?"

"No, I don't. It was some man, and they talked for a while and then the man drove away. "The lights remained on in the office and well, just to check up, I made an excuse to run over to ask him a question, and — well, I'm there now."

"But the lights are on?"

"Yes."

"Evidently then, he intends to come back soon."

"I suppose so, but —"

"If you hadn't been checking up on him," Mason said, "you would have thought he was still there because the lights were on?"

"Yes."

"I don't like that."

"Neither do I. That's why I'm phoning you. It — it looks as though he might be trying to build an alibi for something."

Mason said, "Okay, Patricia. Now don't get panic-stricken. If you need anything, call the Drake Detective Agency. The number is in the book. There'll be someone there all night. If anything happens, call there and tell them who you are."

"I don't want to stay here, Mr. Mason."

"Why?"

"Because, if he should be planning anything . . . I'm a witness . . . You see, I know why Mother left. I don't want to be here alone with him. He's capable of anything. I'm afraid of him."

"He doesn't know about this Las Olitas address of yours?"

"No. No one does; only Mother."

"Okay," Mason said. "Go there. Sit tight. Good night now."

Mason hung up the phone, called the Drake

Detective Agency, got Paul Drake on the line, and said, "Paul, something's going on. I don't know just what it is, but I don't like it."

"What's up, Perry?"

Swiftly he brought Paul Drake up to date.

"Allred's probably not out of town," Drake said. "Otherwise he'd have taken his own car."

"Unless he has one planted somewhere. No news of Mrs. Allred?"

"No."

"You're covering auto camps?"

"All along the road. They could have driven somewhere around three hundred miles since ten o'clock this morning. We're trying to cover the places where they could have holed up for the night."

"What about the near auto courts?"

"What do you mean 'near'?"

"Right around here."

"Have a heart, Perry. There are too many of those. We're picking up the ones within about a hundred miles and . . ."

"We're overlooking a bet," Mason interrupted.

"What do you mean?"

Mason said, "Allred spent Saturday night in the motel in Springfield. He also spent yesterday night in that motel. I have a hunch Mrs. Allred won't stay in a motel with Fleetwood unless her husband is there. That means it has to be someplace within two or three hours' drive. Check the motels in Springfield again. Check the near ones, Paul."

"We can't do it, Perry. There are just too darn many of them around the city, too many different roads that . . ."

"That's all right. Put your Springfield man on the job. Check the courts in Springfield. Check the ones that are on the roads near Springfield."

"Okay," Drake said wearily. "We'll try and do the best we can, Perry."

Mason hung up and began pacing the floor, until after almost an hour, wearied by the sheer physical exertion, he flung himself once more into the big chair under the reading light. He was restless, nervous, and frowning and irritable. Two more hours found him dozing.

The phone rang again.

Mason jerked the receiver from its cradle, said, "Yes, what is it?"

Paul Drake said, "My face is red, Perry."

"Shoot."

"You called a turn. Frankly, the possibility hadn't occurred to me."

"Of the near-by auto camp? You mean you've located them?"

"Yes."

"Where?"

"It's a little place and it's only about thirty-five miles from Springfield. It's up in the mountains, on the road that cuts across the high mountain range and comes down to the desert on the other side. This place is a little auto court known as the Snug-Rest Auto Court. The registration is the same as it was in Springfield, R. G. Fleetwood and sister."

"The accommodations?"

"Double cabin with three beds."

"Mrs. Allred's car there?"

"I don't know, Perry, whether it's there right now or not, but the license number is her license number. It's the party we want, all right."

"Why don't you know whether the car's there now or not, Paul?"

"Because my man isn't up there. He's at Springfield. He couldn't possibly have covered all the different roads except by telephone, and he's been telephoning every auto court asking them to give him a list of reservations that were made any time during the day."

"How long will it take us to get there?"

"Right around three hours, Perry."

"We're on our way!" Mason told him excitedly. "I'll drive down and pick you up. Stick a gun in your pocket."

"Going to take Della?"

"No. The party may be rough."

"Want my man to go up and wait, keeping them under observation?"

"No. He may tip them off. Tell him to stay on the job in Springfield. We may want to call him for something there."

"How soon will you be here?"

"Damn near as soon as *you* can get downstairs," Mason said, hanging up the phone and grabbing his hat and coat from the chair.

His car was parked in front of the apartment building, fully serviced. Mason made time to the office building where Paul Drake, his thin frame wrapped in a heavy overcoat, climbed protestingly into the car.

"For the love of mike, Perry, have a heart! Don't scare me to death getting there; and try to keep four wheels on the ground on some of the curves. That road from Springfield up over the mountains is a humdinger. Ever been over it?"

"Three or four times," Mason said.

"Well, it's a bad one. You go right straight up. You follow a stream for a ways and then zig-zag the side of a canyon until you hit the plateau country on top. It's a damn mean road."

"Then hang on," Mason said. "I'll try to get you there in one piece."

"What's the hurry?" Drake asked.

Mason said, "I have a hunch there's more to this than appears on the surface, Paul. I'm not too certain but what Allred isn't planning to pull a fast one."

"You mean getting a divorce?"

"It might suit him better to be a widower. I understand he has quite a lot of his wife's money invested in mining properties."

"I guess Allred does all right for himself," Drake said. "He seems to have lots of dough."

Mason said, "I'll bet you even money that Allred forged that check for twenty-five hundred bucks that was sent to me."

"Why?"

"That," Mason said, grimly, "is one of the things I intend to ask him."

"You think he's up there in this Snug-Rest Motel?"

"Uh huh," Mason said, and then gave his attention to his driving.

# Chapter 9

"Know the numbers of the cabins, Paul?"

"Yes. Cabins number four and five. There'll be two entrances. Take it easy. We should be almost there."

A sign flashed up in the headlights, gleaming whitely at them out of a cold drizzle, etching its dazzling message on their tired eyes, *"Snug-Rest-Auto Court One Mile."*

As Mason eased the speed of the car, the windshield wipers gathered speed, pulsed hysterically. Drake, straightening up in the seat, heaved a sigh of relief. He watched the figures on the speedometer, said, "You'll have to slow down, Perry. You've gone eight-tenths of a mile since that sign. The place may be hard to see . . . It's a cinch the cabins have all been rented, the lights turned off, and the people who run the place have gone to bed. Here it is, right ahead, Perry."

Mason slammed on the brakes. The car started to skid on the wet road, then righted itself, and Mason turned into the unpretentious little tourist court.

"Take it easy," Drake cautioned. "Cut off your motor as soon as you can locate the numbers. We'll try to do it as quietly as possible. There it is, Perry. There's the cabin, the one over there on the right. Thank heavens, it's off by itself so we won't have an audience."

Mason swung his car to a stop in front of the two-cabin unit that had been erected slightly apart from the other cabins, uniform in their somewhat shabby austerity.

The lawyer switched off the ignition, then the headlights.

Drake opened the car door.

Mason got out on his side, and they stood for a moment in front of the car.

The rain was a localized mountain rain, a cold, cloud-shrouded drizzle. In the background somewhere a stream tumbling over rocks made noisy gossip with the night. Aside from these noises there was nothing for the ears. The auto court was wrapped in silence.

"They've gone to bed," Drake said in a low voice.

Mason said, "I guess we're in time, Paul. That's a break." He climbed the steps and knocked on the door.

There was no answer. He knocked again.

Paul Drake, who had made a quick circle around the cabins on a tour of inspection, came to stand beside Mason. "It's a red herring," he said.

"What's the matter?"

"They aren't here."

"You mean someone else is . . ."

"No. I don't think the cabin's rented at all. There isn't any car under the cabin shed."

Mason tentatively turned the knob on the cabin

105

door. The door was unlocked. The latch clicked and the door swung open, disclosing a dark interior.

Paul Drake said cautiously, "Take it easy, Perry. Someone's in here. That's fresh tobacco smoke. The curtains are all drawn."

"Anyone home?" Mason called.

He was greeted by silence, the dark oblong of the open doorway seeming sinister in its black mystery.

"Someone's here all right," Mason said, as warm air came eddying out from the dark interior of the cabin. "A heater of some sort has been on in here, and that certainly is fresh tobacco smoke."

"Okay, let's back out," Drake whispered, "and go to the office. Let's check the registrations."

"Anyone home?" Mason called again.

Again there was that wall of black, sinister silence.

Mason groped inside the door, running his fingers along the wall searching for a light switch.

"Don't, Perry," Drake begged. "Let's go to the office first and . . ."

Mason clicked on the lights.

The room was empty.

"Come on in," Mason said.

Drake hung back, but finally followed the lawyer into the room.

Mason closed the door. It was a typical tourist cabin in the medium-price range. Mason, looking swiftly around the room, kept up a running fire of comment to Paul Drake.

"Bed has been sat on, but not slept in. Tobacco smoke pretty fresh. Cigarette butts with lipstick on them. Oh, oh, Paul, here's something."

"What?"

Mason indicated a couple of glasses, leaned over to smell them.

"They had some drinks in these glasses," Mason said, "and not very long ago. You can see the ice isn't entirely melted. There's still a spot of ice in the bottom of this glass."

Drake started to reach for the glass. Mason grabbed his wrist, pulled it away, said, "Don't touch anything right now, Paul, but remember there's a speck of ice in one of these glasses. You can smell the odor of whisky."

"There's another room here," Drake said in a low voice. "I still think we're going to run into something, Perry."

Mason opened a door which disclosed a rather dispirited looking kitchen, with a gas stove, a small electric icebox and a cupboard containing a few dishes, virtually the irreducible minimum of frying pan, coffee pot, stewpan, four plates, four cups and saucers.

The lawyer opened a door, which led to a bathroom. There was also a door at the other end of the bathroom, which was closed.

"This goes to the other cabin," Drake said. "Perry, I wish you'd keep out of this until after we've . . ."

The lawyer knocked gently on the closed door from the bathroom.

When there was no answer, he opened the door, stepped into the other room and groped for a light.

"They haven't been in here at all," he said. "This place is cold."

Drake surveyed the empty room, said, "Well, I guess that's it, Perry."

Mason gave a quick look around the room, then closed the door. They walked back to the front cabin, switching out lights as they walked.

Mason said, "Two people. They sat around here for a while, had a couple of drinks, smoked, had the gas wall heater turned on . . . must have been here for quite a little while, Paul. Look at the number of cigarette stubs."

"Suppose they got a tip we were coming?" Drake asked.

Mason shrugged.

"Of course," Drake pointed out, "they could have gone someplace planning to come back."

Mason shook his head. "Not a scrap of baggage anywhere. Let's take a look in the icebox."

Mason returned to the kitchen, opened the door of the icebox, pulled out the tray reserved for ice cubes, said, "Every ice cube taken out, Paul."

He pressed his finger down on the surface of the water in the ice tray. Its thin coating of ice cracked under the pressure of his finger.

"I don't get it," Drake said.

"It means there was more than one highball," Mason explained. "Probably two or three."

Drake said nervously, "I hate to be prowling around in here, Perry. If we get caught . . ."

Mason replaced the tray in the icebox, snapped the door shut, clicked off the lights in the kitchen and said, "I feel the same way, Paul. We're getting out."

"Then what?"

"We're going back. You're going to bed. I'm going to drop you in Las Olitas. You can take a taxicab back to the city. I'm going to talk with Patricia. I think I've been on the receiving end of a fast one."

# Chapter 10

The night garage man at the Westwick Hotel Apartments regarded the ten dollar bill which Mason handed him with eager appraisal.

"Who do you want killed, buddy?" he asked.

"Know anything about Maurine Milford?"

The man grinned. "Why?"

"Just wondering."

"Not much."

"Perhaps whatever it is will help."

"Shucks," the night man said. "I hate to take the money for what little I know, because it isn't worth the ten bucks."

Nevertheless, he folded Mason's bill and pushed it down deep in his pocket.

"You can't ever tell," Mason said. "What is it?"

"The day man told me she slipped him a five buck tip to keep her car shined up and polished. The day man doesn't have anything to do with that stuff. I do the work. The day man offered to split the tip with me, but I told him I thought I could get another five. Well, sure enough, this Milford woman was in the first part of the evening and took her car out. I gave it a few finishing touches. I told her I hadn't had a chance to really work on it, but that I would when she brought it back. I managed to get it across to her that it was

110

the night man that did the work."

"So what?"

The man grinned and said, "A five. Added to your ten, that makes fifteen bucks for the night. That's something!"

"And when did she bring the car back?"

"She hasn't brought it back. Looks like an all night party to me."

Mason said, "What do you do to keep yourself occupied down here?"

"What do I do? Gosh, buddy, I have all these cars to dust off, and the windshields have to be washed. I . . . ."

"And then what do you do when it gets along in the small hours of the morning like this?"

The garage man grinned and said, "After all, ten bucks is ten bucks. I guess there's no reason you and I shouldn't get along. I pick a car that has nice comfortable cushions and a damn good car radio. I park it out where I can see the entrance in case anybody comes in, and turn on the radio and sit there and listen to whatever all night program is on. Some of them are pretty terrible, but it beats standing around on a cold cement floor and biting your fingernails. Then when you see someone coming in, you jump out of the car, switch off the radio, start scrubbing away at the windshield or polishing a fender. Like I was doing when you came in, buddy."

Mason said, "Move over, we'll listen to the radio together."

"What's your racket?" the man asked.

Mason said, "I'm sort of strung for the Milford girl."

"Oh, oh! Beg your pardon, buddy — what I said about an all night party. I don't know her at all, I was just shooting off my face."

"It's okay," Mason said. "What station did you have on?"

"It's some recordings," the man said. "Not bad. They'll come on with a breakfast program in about an hour and a half."

"Disc jockey?"

"Oh, so so. He is pretty crude and amateurish, but he's probably practicing up for daytime stuff. This is a good radio."

Mason climbed in the car and sat with the night man. The radio warmed up and a record of cowboy music filled their ears.

"I like this stuff," the garage man said. "Always wanted to be a cowboy — so I turn up washing off windshields at night. Helluva life!"

"Darned if it isn't," Mason agreed. "Will you have a smoke?"

"I'm sorry, buddy, but I don't smoke in a car. There's always the chance that the man who owns this particular heap might come walking in and . . ."

"Sorry," Mason apologized.

"Get out and walk around when you want to smoke," the man invited. "And then get back . . . oh, oh!"

His hand snaked out, turned off the radio.

"Out," he said out of the side of his mouth, "quick."

Mason opened the car on the right and slid out to the cement floor.

The garage man, with a rag in his hand, was assiduously polishing the fender on the car, as headlights came down the ramp from the street.

The night man put down the rag on the fender, walked across to the automobile, said, "Okay, I've got it."

"Hello," Patricia Faxon said, as she jumped out of the car with a quick, lithe motion. "Guess I was out pretty late, wasn't I?"

The night man merely grinned at her.

"Do the best you can with the car," she said. "It's streaked up a bit. When can I get it washed?"

"Not until tomorrow."

"Well, that's okay. Do the best you can with it. I . . ."

She suddenly stiffened at sight of Perry Mason.

"Hello," the lawyer said.

"What are *you* doing here?"

"I wanted to talk with you."

"How long have you been here?"

Mason merely smiled, said, "Let's do our talking in your apartment, Patricia."

"At this hour?" she asked.

Mason nodded.

She regarded him for a long moment with hesitant appraisal; then she led the way to the elevator shaft and pressed the button.

The elevator was on automatic at this hour of

113

the night, and it responded promptly.

Mason held the door open for her. She entered the cage. Mason followed her. The door slid shut and Patricia pushed the button for the eighth floor.

Mason said, "I thought you were the frightened girl who couldn't get back here fast enough."

"I changed my mind."

"What caused you to change your mind?"

She pretended not to hear him. The elevator stopped at the eighth floor. They walked down the corridor together. Patricia fitted a latchkey to the door, said, "I suppose you know you're kicking my good name out of the window."

Mason didn't say anything.

She switched on lights in the apartment. Mason closed the door.

She said, "I'm going to fix myself a drink. A big one. What do you want?"

"What are you having?"

"Scotch and soda."

"Okay by me. Where have you been, Pat?"

"Out."

Mason said, "We might get farther if you'd be more co-operative."

She laughed breezily and said, "I've heard that before somewhere. Believe it or not, I just drove out here from our house in the city."

Mason followed her out into the kitchenette. She took a bottle of Scotch from the shelf, then took out two glasses; then she took ice cubes from the refrigerator.

"Been drizzling up in the mountains," the lawyer said. "Rather nasty weather."

"Is that so?"

"And," the lawyer went on, "I noticed that your car was pretty much a mess. Evidently you've had it out where it's wet."

She splashed Scotch into the glasses without bothering with the jigger measure that was on the shelf by the Scotch bottle.

"See your mother?" Mason asked.

She said, "You'll find soda in the icebox, Mr. Mason."

"See your mother?" he repeated, taking a siphon of soda water from the refrigerator.

"I think I want to let this drink take effect before I do any talking at all."

"What's the matter?" the lawyer asked. "Something to conceal?"

She made no answer, but led the way back to the living room, took a quick drink from the glass, said, "What's this going to be, the third-degree?"

"Not unless it has to be. I want to know whether you saw your mother."

"I . . ."

Knuckles tapped gently on the panel of the door. For one panic-stricken second, Patricia pretended not to hear them. Then the chimes sounded and Mason said casually, "Do you want to open the door, Pat, or shall I?"

Without a word, she put her drink on the stand by her chair, walked across and opened the door.

A woman's voice said, "Thank heavens, you're up, Pat. I . . ."

She broke off at the sight of Mason.

For a moment, she and Pat faced each other. Then the elder woman said, "I'm sorry. I guess I have the wrong apartment. I . . ."

"Come on in, Mrs. Allred," Mason said. "One would hardly take you for Pat's mother. You look more like her sister."

She smiled and said, "It's a nice opening line. I've heard it before. Aren't you keeping Pat up rather late?"

Mason said, "It isn't a line and it isn't flattery. You might call it a professional appraisal of an article of merchandise I may have to sell to a jury."

Patricia closed the door. "Perry Mason, Mother."

*"Oh!"* she said in a single sharp exclamation.

"We're having a drink," Patricia went on. "You must be cold."

"I'm numb," her mother admitted.

"I'll fix you one."

Mrs. Allred smiled vaguely at Mason, hesitated a moment, then followed her daughter into the kitchen.

"Have any trouble getting in?" Patricia asked.

She said, "The night man at the desk was a little dubious, but I flashed him a smile and walked directly to the elevator with all of the assurance in the world. He finally decided I belonged here."

"There's ice there in the refrigerator, Mother. You want Bourbon and soda?"

"That's right."

Mason could hear the gurgle of liquid, the clink of ice in a glass, then the sibilants of swift whispers.

The lawyer settled back in his chair, lit a cigarette, inhaled deeply, arose politely when the two women reentered the room.

"Got it all fixed up?" Mason asked.

"What?" Patricia asked. "The drink?"

"No. The story."

Patricia glared at him. Both women sat down.

Mason said, "You can beat around the bush if you want to. I don't know how much time we have."

Patricia said, "I told Mr. Mason about Bob Fleetwood, Mother. He knows how things are."

Mrs. Allred said, "After all, Mr. Mason, I have nothing to conceal. I found accommodations at a little tourist camp up in the mountains. I had previously telephoned my husband where we would be, and he said he was coming up to join us."

"Did he?"

She hesitated.

"Go on," Mason said. "Let's hear the story."

She said, "Bob and I had a couple of drinks, killing time and waiting. Then Bob excused himself to go to the bathroom. He was in there quite a while. After a while I called to him to find out if he was all right. There was no answer. The door was locked from the inside.

"I was in a panic. I thought perhaps he'd taken something, or — well, you know, it could have been suicide."

"But it wasn't?"

"He had the key to the other cabin. I ran around to try the outside door of that cabin. It was open. The bathroom door on that side was open. He hadn't stopped in the bathroom at all. He'd locked the door to my side, walked right on through, gone out the other door, taken my car and driven away."

"Didn't you hear your car when it drove away?" Mason asked.

"I heard it, but thought it was some other tenant. I didn't have any idea it was my car. I'd left it parked in the driveway."

"Where did he go?"

"I don't know."

"What did you do?"

"I walked out to the road," she said, "and hitchhiked in. I don't want to have that experience again."

"How about your luggage?"

She said, "I had a small suitcase with me. I'd taken it out because there was a flask of whisky in it. We were waiting for Bertrand to join us."

"Did Fleetwood know that?"

"Yes."

"Had he recovered his memory?"

"No. He was all right otherwise, but he hadn't recovered his memory."

"And what about your husband?"

"I don't know what happened to him, Mr. Mason. He never did show up."

"You didn't wait to find out, did you?"

"He was long overdue when Bob took the car. I . . . well, I don't know what happened."

"Did you try calling your house?"

"Yes. Of course."

"What happened?"

"There was no answer."

"No servants?"

"They sleep over the garage. They wouldn't answer a phone at night."

"So then you went out to the highway and hitchhiked back?"

"Yes."

"Get the name of the motorist who took you in?"

"Motorists," she said, making an exaggerated "s" sound.

"That s-s-s-s-s stands for plural. There were three of them in succession. The last man was an old man."

"Did he drive you directly here?"

"No. He got me in to where I could get a taxicab, however."

"And your suitcase? Were you lying about leaving it in the car?"

"I left it at the depot. I checked it because I thought I might have some trouble getting in here with a suitcase. I thought I could walk in and get to Pat's apartment all right, if I didn't have a suitcase. If I did have, I knew I'd be stopped and have to make explanations."

"Why didn't you want to explain?"

"I wasn't ready."

"Why didn't you go home?"

"Because I . . . because I was afraid to."

"Why?"

"I don't know. It was just a hunch I had. I wanted to be with Pat."

"You telephoned your husband earlier in the evening and told him where you would be?"

"That's right."

"And he was to come right up?"

"As soon as he could get away. He said he'd be up about ten o'clock."

"And how about Pat?"

"What about her?"

"Did you telephone her?"

For a moment, there was silence.

Mason said, "Of course, the police will check the calls."

"What do the police have to do with it?"

"I don't know," Mason said, and then added significantly, "yet."

"I don't see where it needs to concern the police at all."

"How many drinks had Fleetwood had?"

"A couple. We didn't start drinking until after dinner. I guess it was about nine o'clock when we started drinking."

"Were they loaded pretty heavy?"

"He seemed to be pretty thirsty," she admitted.

"I held him down as much as I could."

"How big a flask?"

"A pint."

"Any left in it?"

"No."

"Did you telephone Pat?"

"Yes."

"Ask Pat to come up?"

"Yes."

"Why?"

"Because I . . . I wasn't certain that what I was doing was for the best. I wanted to have a showdown."

"Tell your husband that over the telephone?"

"No. I didn't phone Pat until nine o'clock, just before the office at the Snug-Rest closed up. Bob stole my car shortly after I called."

"What did you tell Pat over the phone?"

"Just where I was, is all."

"Ask her to come up?"

"Not directly."

Mason looked at Patricia.

"I tried to call you," she said. "You didn't answer."

"And why didn't you call the Drake Detective Agency?"

"I thought I'd have a talk with Mother first."

"Did you?"

"The cabin was empty when I got there."

"You went in?"

"Yes."

Mason turned to Mrs. Allred. "How long did

it take you to get here?"

"I don't know. I guess it was hours. Sometimes car after car would go by without stopping. Then the people who did stop seemed to want to go up side roads. It was an experience I wouldn't want to repeat. I'm a little hazy on the time element."

"Yes," Mason said drily, "I can see you are. You both are."

Mason walked across to the telephone and was just about to pick up the receiver, when knuckles pounded on the door of the apartment.

"Good heavens," Mrs. Allred said. "Who's that?"

The knuckles pounded again, harder, more authoritatively.

Mason said, swiftly, "Both of you get this. Don't do any talking. Let me do the talking."

"But won't it be worse if we don't explain?"

"Don't say anything," Mason warned. "Let me do the talking."

The chimes sounded, and again there was the sound of knuckles. Mason walked across and opened the door.

Lieutenant Tragg of the city homicide squad and Frank Inman of the sheriff's office seemed far more surprised to see Mason than the lawyer was to see them.

"Come in," Mason invited.

"What the hell," Tragg said.

Mason said, "Mrs. Allred, this is Frank Inman of the sheriff's office, and Lieutenant Tragg of the homicide squad. Gentlemen, this is Mrs. Bertrand C. Allred and her daughter, Patricia Faxon. Miss Faxon has rented this apartment under the name of Maurine Milford, because she is intending to become an authoress. She wanted a place where she could write without being disturbed."

"Mrs. Allred, eh? Well, well, well," Lieutenant Tragg said sarcastically. "And we have a Master of Ceremonies too! Suppose you let the women do the talking for a while, Mason."

"Mrs. Allred has a cold," Mason said, "and her daughter has a slight impediment of speech. Suppose you do the talking first."

Tragg said, "You're sure this is Mrs. Allred, Mason?"

"Her daughter should be sure."

Tragg said to Mrs. Allred, "You ran away with Bob Fleetwood, didn't you, Mrs. Allred?"

She started to answer the question.

Mason held up his hand, said, "Tut, tut, gentlemen. Can't we be more diplomatic?"

Inman said, "What the hell are you doing in this, anyway?"

Tragg said, "He's the mouthpiece. The fact he's here at all is the best indication of guilt I know."

Mason laughed and said, "As a matter of fact, I'm here on a civil case."

"How do you know *we* aren't?" Inman demanded.

"Merely from the personnel," Mason said. "Suppose you tell us what's happened?"

"We'd like to have some questions answered first."

Mason said, "We're allergic to questions until we know what happened."

Inman said, "What the hell! I can take these women down and throw them in the hoosegow if I have to."

"Sure you can," Mason said, "and I can get a writ of *habeas corpus* if I have to."

Tragg said, "This isn't getting us anywhere. All right, if you want it the hard way, we'll take it the hard way. When did you see Bob Fleetwood last, Mrs. Allred?"

"I . . . I . . ."

"Find out the reason for the question before you answer it, Mrs. Allred," Mason said.

Tragg flushed. "All right, I'll give you the reason for the question. Mrs. Allred's automobile was found down at the bottom of a canyon on a mountain road. Bob Fleetwood was in it, and he was quite dead. Now suppose you do some talking, Mrs. Allred."

"Bob Fleetwood dead!" she exclaimed.

"That's what I said."

"Take it easy," Mason cautioned.

"Why," she exclaimed, "he must have had too much to drink, then. He . . ."

"What was he doing driving your car in the first place?"

She said, "I don't know. He simply took my car and drove away."

"Without your permission?"

Mason stepped behind Tragg, frowned at her, and placed a finger to his lips.

She said, "That must explain everything. He was trying to get away. I thought he was suffering from amnesia, but I knew it might be just a gag. I told him I was his sister and he seemed to believe that and seemed perfectly willing to wait for his mind to clear."

"This is a hell of a mixed up statement," Inman said.

Tragg motioned him to silence and glanced significantly at Perry Mason. "We're lucky to get anything," he said, in a low voice.

Mrs. Allred said somewhat defiantly, "Mr. Mason, under the circumstances, I don't see why we should run the risk of being misunderstood. I think that these people are entitled to a frank statement of what happened. Mr. Fleetwood was suffering from amnesia. I tried to bring him back to familiar surroundings by posing as his sister. I told him my husband was his brother-in-law. We thought that would keep him quiet and keep him from worrying, and would give his mind a chance to clear.

"We were staying at a motor court, and I was waiting for my husband. I had a flask of whisky and Bob Fleetwood had several drinks. He kept loading them pretty heavy. I tried to get him to stop, but he stayed with it until he emptied the flask."

"You drink anything?" Lieutenant Tragg asked.

"I drank just as much as I felt that I could. I knew that after he got started, Bob was going to empty the flask, and I didn't want him to do that. I mean I didn't want him to get tight. I knew that every drop that I drank would leave that much less for him. I . . ."

"How many drinks did you have?"

"I had two. He had three."

"Then what?"

"Then he took my car and started back to town."

"Without your permission?"

"Yes."

"Without your knowledge?"

"Yes."

"And then what happened?"

"That's all I know, but if he had an accident — well, it was on account of the liquor he'd been drinking. You can check that in some way, can't you? Can't you analyze his blood and find out?"

"Sure, we can," Lieutenant Tragg said, "but we'd like to know a few things first."

"What?"

"Well, in the first place," Tragg said, "we came up here on sort of a blind lead. The officers who investigated the automobile accident found a key to these tourist cabins in the car. They went up to the tourist cabins and found they were empty. Then they got the manager out of bed and she told them about renting the cabin to Fleetwood and his sister and said you'd put through a couple of calls from the office just before the place closed up. The boys checked the numbers of those calls. One of them was to the Allred residence and the other one was here. They phoned us to investigate. There was no one at the Allred residence, so we came up here. We hardly expected to find you."

"Well, I can explain everything. That's exactly the way it happened."

"Is it customary for the homicide squad to investigate automobile accidents?" Mason asked drily.

"Shut up, wise guy," Inman said.

Tragg kept his eyes on Mrs. Allred, held her attention so that she failed to appreciate the significance of the lawyer's remark.

"And you think Bob Fleetwood drove your car off the road?"

"I'm quite certain he did."

"You think he was drunk?"

"He'd been drinking. I didn't think he was drunk. No. But if he drove the car off the road, he must have been."

"Well," Tragg said, "there are a couple more things you'd better explain. One of them was why the car was locked in low gear when it was driven off the road."

Mason said, "After all, Mrs. Allred, why don't you wait until you *know* exactly what Tragg wants, before you . . ."

"Don't try to lock the stable door after the horse has been stolen," Tragg said.

Mason said, "I merely wanted to . . ."

"And while you're explaining that," Tragg said, "you might also explain how it happens that there's blood on the carpet of the luggage compartment in your automobile."

"Blood on the luggage compartment in *my* automobile?" she asked incredulously.

"That's right."

"Why, I . . . I haven't the faintest idea how . . . you're sure?"

"Of course, I'm sure."

"I . . ."

Knuckles tapped on the door of the apartment.

Frank Inman opened it.

A plain-clothes officer stepped inside and said to Tragg, "Lieutenant, may I talk with you a moment? There's some additional information just came in over the police radio in the car."

Tragg stepped out in the corridor. Inman said to Mason, "As far as I'm concerned, we can get along without you."

Mason merely smiled.

Lieutenant Tragg came back and said, "I'm sorry, Mrs. Allred. I made a mistake."

He was watching her with narrowed eyes.

"You mean there wasn't an automobile accident? You mean my car didn't go over the grade?"

"No," Tragg said. "I mean that there was an accident. I mean that your car did go over the grade. I mean that there's a dead man locked in

128

the car, and I mean the car was deliberately driven over the grade in low gear. The thing I made the mistake on was the identity of the body. When the police made the first identification, they got off wrong because they found a billfold containing a driving license, social security number and a few other things belonging to Robert Gregg Fleetwood; but after a while they also uncovered a billfold of someone else, and when they saw the descriptions they came to the conclusion that the dead man had been carrying Fleetwood's billfold, but wasn't Fleetwood at all."

"Then who was he?" Mrs. Allred asked.

Tragg snapped the information at her as though he had been turning the words into bullets, "Your husband, Bertrand C. Allred," he said. Now tell us how he got in your car and was driven off the grade."

"Why, I . . . I . . ."

"And how blood got over the carpet in the luggage compartment of your automobile."

She hesitated. Her eyes wide with tragic appeal, she looked at Mason.

Frank Inman saw the glance. He stepped forward and took Mason's arm. "And as far as you're concerned," he said to the lawyer, "this is where you came in and this is where you go out. Hold everything, Lieutenant."

Tragg said, "I'd like an answer to that question now."

Inman, taking Mason's arm, pushed him out toward the corridor.

129

Mason said, "You can't keep me from advising my client."

"The hell I can't," Inman said. "I can put you out of here, and if you get rough I'll get a damn sight rougher."

Mason said over his shoulder, "Mrs. Allred, your rights are being curtailed. As your lawyer, I advise you to say absolutely nothing until the officers cease these highhanded methods. I want your silence not to be considered as any indication of guilt, or because you're afraid anything you say might incriminate you, but simply as a protest against the highhanded and illegal methods of these police officers."

Lieutenant Tragg said irritably to Inman, "You've done it, now. You've given him a chance to make a speech and make a good excuse."

"I don't give a damn," Inman said. "That woman's either going to explain about her dead husband, or she's going to be put under arrest."

Mason said, "You can always reach me at my office, Mrs. Allred, or through the Drake Detective Agency."

"Come on," Tragg said, "we're going to take a ride. Both of you women are going to headquarters."

Inman pushed Mason out into the corridor, pulled the door of the apartment shut.

Mason walked down the corridor, took the elevator down to the lobby and said to the sleepy night clerk, "Where's the phone booth?"

The night clerk regarded him curiously. "You live here?" he asked.

"No," Mason said. "I'm an investor. I'm thinking of buying this hotel merely as an investment. How much do you suppose I should raise wages in order to get courtesy from the employees?"

The night clerk smiled dubiously, said, "The telephone booth is over there, in the corner."

Mason went over and phoned Paul Drake's office.

"Where's Paul?" he asked the night operator.

"He went home and went to bed, said not to disturb him for anything short of murder."

Mason grinned. "Okay, ring him up. Tell him that you're following his instructions to the letter."

"What do you mean?"

Mason said, "I mean that Bertrand C. Allred was murdered up on the mountain grade above Springfield. Then he was locked up in Mrs. Allred's car, the car put in low gear and driven down over a steep grade. Drake has a man in Springfield. Tell him to get that man on the phone and have him start up there in a hurry. I want information, I want photographs and I want Fleetwood. You get that all down?"

"Yes, Mr. Mason. Do you want to talk with Mr. Drake?"

"Not now," Mason said. "I'm working on another angle of the case and I don't want to be tied up in a telephone booth when the time comes for action."

He hung up, left the telephone booth, strolled to the door of the lobby, and looked out.

It was getting daylight. The sun was not up as yet, and the street outside showed cold and gray in the colorless light of dawn.

A police car with red spotlight and siren was parked at the curb. The radio antenna was stretched to its full capacity. The plain-clothes officer who had taken the message to Lieutenant Tragg was seated behind the wheel. The motor was running, and little puffs of white smoke put-put-put-put-put-putted from the end of the exhaust.

Mason stood there looking out of the door for a matter of some five minutes. The light strengthened. The objects on the street began to show color.

Mason glanced at his wrist watch, stretched, yawned, and strolled over to glance at the indicator of the automatic elevator. It was still on the eighth floor.

The lawyer pressed the button which brought the elevator back down to the ground floor. He opened the door just far enough to break the electrical contact and kept the door from closing by inserting a pencil between the door and the door jamb. He then took a seat in the lobby, near the elevator.

Another ten minutes, and Mason heard a faint buzzing from the interior of the elevator, indicating that someone was trying to put it in service.

He walked over, removed the pencil from the

door, opened the door, got in the elevator and let the spring on the door pull the door shut. As soon as the door snapped into position, the mechanism of the elevator gave a sharp, metallic click, and the cage started rumbling upward.

Mason stood over in the corner where he would be out of sight to anyone opening the door.

The cage lumbered up to the eighth floor, came to a stop.

The doors were opened. Inman pushed Mrs. Allred and Patricia into the elevator, followed them in. Tragg entered the elevator and closed the door. Inman said, "And if your lawyer is waiting in the lobby, don't try to talk with him. You get me?"

They turned to face the door, and Mrs. Allred gasped as she saw Mason.

Inman jerked his head at the sound of the gasp. His hand started streaking for his gun. Then he stopped the motion midway to his holster.

"Ground floor?" Mason asked, and promptly pressed the button.

The cage started rumbling down to the ground floor.

Tragg said drily to Inman, "I told you he was smart."

"What have you told them?" Mason asked Mrs. Allred.

"Shut up," Inman said.

"Nothing at all," Mrs. Allred said. "I followed instructions."

"Keep on following them," Mason said.

133

"They'll try everything in their power to make you talk. Simply tell them that your silence is a protest against their highhanded methods and that you want to have an interview with your attorney before you say anything. Remember that you were making a full and frank statement of everything that had happened until they became arbitrary and started pushing me around."

Inman said, "It's a big temptation to *really* start pushing you around!"

"Don't lose your temper," Mason told Inman. "It runs up your blood pressure and makes your face look like hell."

Tragg said wearily, "Don't be a damn fool, Inman! He's *trying* to get you to start something. It'll sound like hell in front of a jury."

Inman lapsed into sullen silence.

The cage lurched to a stop at the ground floor.

Mason opened the door, said, "Ground floor, ladies and gentlemen. Department of frame-ups just ahead of you — separate cells, phony confessions, telling the daughter her mother's confessed, telling the mother the daughter's confessed, throwing in stool pigeons and detectives as cell mates, and all the usual police traps, right this way!"

Inman pushed the women out into the lobby, turned back toward Mason, suddenly cocked his fist.

Lieutenant Tragg grabbed his arm.

The officers marched the women across the lobby to the police car, and drove away.

Mason sighed wearily, walked across the street to where he had left his own car parked, climbed in and started the motor.

# Chapter 11

Mason unlocked the door of his private office, entered, nodded to Della, scaled his hat toward the shelf of the hat closet, walked over to his desk and sat down.

"Didn't you sleep at all?" Della Street asked.

Mason shook his head. "Anything from Drake?"

"Yes. He's had a man up at the wreck and has some photographs. This man knew the highway police who were in charge, and he picked up about all the information there was."

"How did they happen to find the car?"

"At the point where the car was driven off the road, there was a guard rail."

"A hell of a place to pick to send a car off the road," Mason said. "Car pretty badly smashed?"

"Smashed to kindling," Della said.

Mason said, "Get Paul Drake in here."

Della Street said, "Dixon Keith is waiting out there. He's been waiting for a while. He was in the corridor when we opened the office."

"Dixon Keith?" Mason asked.

"The one who has the fraud suit against All-red."

"Okay," Mason said, "get Drake first. Then go out and soothe Dixon Keith so he'll wait. Tell him I've phoned and expected to be in in just a few minutes. I don't want him to leave."

Mason settled back in the chair, stroked his forehead with his fingertips. Della Street put through a call to Paul Drake, said, "He'll be right in, Chief. Did you have breakfast?"

"Breakfast and a shave," Mason said. "A hot bath and clean clothes. Did the police find a gun on Allred's body by any chance?"

"I don't know," Della Street said. "I . . . here's Paul Drake!"

Drake's code knock sounded on the door of the office.

Mason nodded to Della Street. She opened the door, and Drake, gaunt and haggard, with stubble rough on his jaw, entered the room and surveyed Mason bleakly.

Mason grinned. "You look as though you've been busy."

"I have."

"I thought you told me that you kept an electric razor in your office so you could shave in between phone calls."

"I do," Drake said. "I have. But, what the hell? I haven't had any time between phone calls. I've been busy!"

"Give."

Drake said, "The place where the car went off the road was within five miles of the Snug-Rest Auto Court. It's the worst place anywhere along the road, and the road is bad enough, at that. There's a guard rail. The car had plowed right through the guard rail. No wonder! It had been locked in low gear and the hand throttle pulled all the way out. The police were able to determine that much from what was left of the car."

"The body was first identified as that of Fleetwood?"

"That's right."

"Allred had Fleetwood's billfold?"

"He had Fleetwood's billfold, cigarette case, fountain pen. Quite a bit of stuff."

"Any explanation?"

"No explanation."

"And there was a key to the Snug-Rest Auto Court?"

"That's right. A key to Fleetwood's cabin."

"How did Allred get that?"

"No explanation so far, Perry. The key was loose in the car."

"There was blood on the carpet of the luggage compartment?"

"That's right."

"Did Allred have a gun?"

"No."

Mason said, "Paul, I want to find Fleetwood!"

Drake's laugh was sarcastic. "Who doesn't?"

"I want to find him just a little worse than anyone else wants to find him."

"When you find him, he'll be dead."

Mason said, "We have an inside track on one thing, Paul."

"What?"

"Fleetwood is either suffering from amnesia or was pretending to suffer from amnesia. If it's a genuine case of amnesia, he'll still be wandering around in a daze. If it's a gag, I think Fleetwood will try keeping it up."

"Unless he's dead," Drake said.

"Someone," Mason said, "drove that car off the grade. What time did it happen, Paul?"

"The clock on the dashboard says eleven-ten. Allred's wrist watch says eleven-ten."

"That, of course, could have been fixed. The watches could have been set ahead."

"Or behind," Drake said.

Mason nodded.

"What does Fleetwood's amnesia have to do with it?"

Mason said, "You have men up there, Paul?"

"Have I got men up there!" Drake said wearily. "I'll say I've got men up there. They're spotted around at every telephone, phoning in such information as they're able to pick up, and standing by for instructions."

Mason said, "I want to try side roads, Paul. I want the places where a man could wander off the main highway. Do you know if Fleetwood knows the country at all?"

"He should," Drake said. "It was up there that Allred and Fleetwood put through that mining deal there was trouble about, the one where they sold a controlling interest in the mine, then got the stockholders to believe there had been some skulduggery and . . ."

"I know all about that," Mason said. "So that was up in this country, was it? And Fleetwood was Allred's right-hand man at the time?"

"Yes."

"Then he must be familiar with the country. All right. Cover every side road," Mason ordered.

"The police theory," Drake said, "is that Fleetwood started hitchhiking and is probably five hundred miles away by this time — unless he's dead. There's an idea on the part of some of the detectives that Fleetwood's body will be found not over three or four hundred yards from the Snug-Rest Auto Court."

"No chance that this thing was an accident?" Mason asked.

"You mean Allred?"

"Yes."

"Hell, no. The thing was typical. The killer made the same mistake such people always make. In place of leaving the car in high gear the way it would have been if the thing had been accidental, the killer left the car in low gear. Whoever it was, stood on the running board, pointed the car for the precipice, pulled the hand throttle all the way out, and stepped off the running board. The car roared down the slope, hurtled off into space and undoubtedly made a beautiful crash seconds later."

"Any bullet holes in the body?"

"No. Apparently he was killed by having been beaten over the head."

"Or hitting his head when the car went over the grade?"

"Probably he was dead before that. The

autopsy surgeon seems to think he was."

"How long before?"

"The autopsy surgeon isn't sticking his neck out, but I gather he wouldn't be too much surprised if Allred had been dead for an hour or so before the car went over the grade."

"When did they discover it?"

"Around three o'clock in the morning. The traffic officers went to the Snug-Rest Auto Court as soon as they found the door key to a cabin there in the car. With those telephone calls it didn't take long to get the lead on that apartment at Las Olitas."

"If Mrs. Allred had been planning murder," Mason said, "she'd hardly have left as broad a clue as that!"

"You can't tell," Drake said. "My hunch is, Perry, that the police are right. Either Fleetwood is dead, or else he's making tracks. My best guess is he's on an airplane right this minute, or else dead as a herring."

"That amnesia business may be a big thing," Mason said. "He's already laid the foundation for it. It's what I'd do under those circumstances. Go ahead and cover the Springfield territory, every ranch, every house, Paul."

"Okay, if you say so."

"And in case they should find him," Mason said, "tell them not to tip their hand at all. Just beat it to a phone and let us know. That other detective agency still on the job, Paul?"

"I'll say it is, but the boys evidently aren't covering the local angles. They're looking for Fleetwood the same places the police are."

"That's always a mistake," Mason grinned. "Okay, Paul, get started."

Drake left the office and Mason nodded to Della Street. "Let's see what Dixon Keith wants, Della."

Dixon Keith, an alert, square-shouldered chap in the late thirties, had dark, restless eyes, dark hair that was beginning to thin at the temples, and the quick springy steps of an athlete. His legs were short, but he had broad shoulders and a thick chest.

He wasted no time in coming to the point.

"Mason," he said, "I guess you know about me."

Mason nodded.

"I'm having a lawsuit with Bertrand Allred and George Jerome. They're a couple of high-powered crooks who have been getting by with murder. I've found out a lot about them since I've engaged in a little business deal with them."

"And you have a lawyer who is representing you?"

"Yes."

"Don't you think it would be better for you to have your lawyer with you when you come here?"

Keith shook his head. "I can tell you what I want in very few words, Mr. Mason. It's purely a business proposition. It isn't a legal matter at all. It's straight business."

"What is it?"

142

"You and I are both over twenty-one, Mr. Mason. We know that no one gets something for nothing. I want something. I'm prepared to give something."

"What do you want, and what are you prepared to give," Mason asked, "bearing in mind that my primary duty is to my client?"

"That's right. You're representing Mrs. Allred, and unless I miss my guess, she's in a jam."

"Indeed?" Mason said, raising his eyebrows.

Keith said, "Look, Mason, let's not kid each other. You have your detective agency working on this case. I have my detective agency working on the case. You've got a damn good detective agency and I've got a damn good detective agency. I don't know how much you know and you don't know how much I know, but we wouldn't be paying out good money for detectives unless we were getting *something*. Right?"

Mason smiled, "Right!"

"Bertrand Allred's body was found in his wife's car. The car was driven over a rocky precipice and was left in low gear — a dead giveaway. It's a little difficult to do a job like that and leave the car in high gear, but it *can* be done."

"You talk as though you'd tried it," Mason said.

"I did a little experimenting," Keith admitted, "in order to find out what a person would have to do to put a car over a slope like that. You can start it running in low gear, open the door, jump to the running board and get away pretty easy.

But when you shift into high gear, then you have a problem on your hands. If there's a steep enough slope for the car to run off the highway through the brush, the car gets to going pretty fast before you can bail out. The best way is to put the car into high gear, turn the ignition on, put on the emergency brake, then get out, take off the emergency brake and let the car start rolling. As the car gathers momentum, since it's in gear it starts turning the motor, and that starts the engine running. Then if the hand throttle is on a little bit, the car really shoots ahead."

"Too bad you couldn't have told the murderer about that," Mason said.

"It is for a fact," Keith admitted. "Leaving the car in low gear was a technical error. That means you're going to have a little tougher job than you would have had otherwise."

"Assuming that my client is a murderer."

"Assuming that your client will be *accused* of murder," Keith said. "You know it and I know it."

Mason said, "You seem to have given this a good deal of thought."

"This thing is going to concern me," Keith admitted. "I have to find Robert Gregg Fleetwood."

"I understand quite a few people are looking for him."

"Let's not beat around the bush, Mason. You want him because you think that if you find him and get a statement from him, you may get something that will help your client. I want him because if I find him and get a statement from him, I can win my lawsuit. Furthermore, I can straighten out a lot of things.

"Fleetwood has for some time been Allred's right-hand man. Allred hatches up the schemes and Fleetwood helps put them into execution. Fleetwood has a lot of admiration for Bertrand Allred and would do damn near anything Allred told him to.

"From all I can find out about Fleetwood, he wanted to get ahead in the world. He had the idea that you didn't get ahead by being too damn altruistic. If you wanted things out of the world, you went out and got them. Otherwise, you didn't get them. Allred inculcated that philosophy in him.

"Now if Fleetwood wants to talk, and I think perhaps he may want to talk, he can tell a lot. The things he'll tell are things I want to hear, but I want to hear them *first.*

"I'm going to make you a proposition. You want to get hold of Fleetwood before anyone else gets hold of him. If you find Fleetwood, I feel sure you'll talk with him about the thing that you want to know about. Then you'll turn him over to the police.

"That's where my proposition comes in. I'll pay you well *not* to turn him over to the police, but to turn him over to me."

Mason grinned. "You have detectives working on the job. You admit you've found out quite a good deal. Now suppose you get hold of him

145

before I do. Will you turn him over to me? After you've got a statement from him?"

Keith shook his head determinedly.

"Why not?"

"Because I want the good will of the police. I can make quite a grandstand if I can turn Fleetwood over to the police. After I get a statement from him, I want to be damned certain that statement isn't changed in any way. I think perhaps the police can help me there a little bit."

"So you want me to play ball with you, but you won't play ball with me?"

Keith didn't hesitate for a minute. "That's quite right."

Mason merely smiled.

"On the other hand, Mr. Mason, I have inducements which I can offer."

"Money?"

"Money."

"How much?"

"Quite a bit. A certain amount for being put in touch with Fleetwood, and a further amount if he can answer some of the questions I want answered."

"What are they?"

"I'll leave you a list. I'll leave you a list that will contain the answers that I hope Fleetwood will give, the answers that will be to my advantage."

Mason shook his head and laughed.

"What's wrong with that?" Keith asked.

"Everything's wrong with it," Mason said. "You want me to act as a sort of a coach for Fleetwood."

"I don't see what you mean."

"The hell you don't. You'll give me a certain, rather modest, amount for putting you in touch with Fleetwood. You'll give me quite a bit more money in the event he answers questions the way you'll want them answered. You'll leave me the list of the questions and a list of the answers you want Fleetwood to give. I'd be a damn poor lawyer if I didn't realize that it was to my advantage to have Fleetwood answer the questions just that way, and it would be quite a temptation in running over the list with him to try and see that he *did* answer them that way."

"Well, what's wrong with that? It's done every day. Whenever any lawyer takes a suit, he knows what answers the witnesses are supposed to give if he's going to win that suit."

Mason said, "The discussion is academic, anyway, because when I get hold of Fleetwood, I'm going to take him to the police myself. That's in case the police want him."

"You can get one thousand dollars by turning him over to me."

"Okay," Mason said grinning. "The line forms at the right."

Keith's eyes narrowed. He studied Mason thoughtfully for a few seconds, then said, "That should have occurred to me earlier. Mason, I want to be sure that if there's any line that forms at the right, I'm starting at the head of it."

"So I gathered."

"All right, just so you know. I'll top any other

bid," Keith said and walked out.

Mason got up and started pacing the office floor, swinging rhythmically back and forth, his thumbs pushed into the armholes of his vest, his head bowed in concentration.

Della Street was watching him silently when the phone on Mason's desk rang. She picked up the instrument.

"Hello . . . yes, Paul . . . okay . . . All right, hang on to the line; I'll tell him." Della looked over at Mason, "Drake says there are detectives watching the office here. He says he thinks they are employed by Dixon Keith and that the idea is that if you should start out of here in a hurry, the detectives will figure you're going to get Fleetwood and will tag along behind."

Mason laughed. "I'd already anticipated that. Let me talk with Paul." Mason picked up the telephone, said, "Hello, Paul. I'm going to leave the office. I'll shake the shadows and establish headquarters where the shadows can't pick me up.

"You stick in your office and wait for my call. I think this man Fleetwood is a lot more important than anyone realizes."

"Okay," Drake said, "but what are you going to do if you locate him, Perry? Think you can make him talk?"

"I'll try to make him talk," Mason said, "but I'll sew him up first."

"Suppose he doesn't want to go with you?"

"I'll make him. I think I know how it can be done."

"Well, that's your funeral," Drake said. "There are penalties for kidnapping, you know."

"I know," Mason said. "I read a law book once."

Drake laughed, "Watch your step, Perry. This is going to get pretty hot."

Mason hung up the phone and said to Della Street, "I want to ditch those detectives, Della, and I want to do it in such a way it will never occur to them that I deliberately ditched them. Get Gertie in here, will you? Tell her to lock the outer door. We'll close up the office."

Della Street nodded, glided out of the office, and a few moments later returned with Gertie, the big, affable, somewhat overweight receptionist.

Mason said, "I want you to do something for me."

"Anything," she said.

"How would you like to act the part of a married woman for a while?"

Gertie grinned. "What is this, Mr. Mason, a proposal or a proposition?"

"A proposition."

"They all are," Gertie said. "Tell me what I'm supposed to do."

"I'm hoping we can locate a man by the name of Fleetwood. He either is an amnesia victim or he's pretending to be an amnesia victim. I'm rather anxious to find out which."

Gertie nodded.

"The police are looking for Fleetwood, and at

least one other private detective agency is looking for him. The man is hotter than a stovelid.

"Now then, the play is to get Fleetwood where he is entirely in our control. That isn't going to be easy. Fleetwood isn't going to want to play. If it really is amnesia, he's going to need convincing. If he has been faking, he's not going to like any part of it. But a man who is pretending amnesia is exceedingly vulnerable."

"How?" Della asked.

"If you tell him anything about his past life, he isn't in any position to contradict you."

Della Street's face lit up as Mason's idea impressed itself upon her. "Then you mean that Gertie . . ."

Mason grinned.

"What's this bird like?" Gertie demanded.

"I think he's quite a wolf, Gertie. Long eyelashes, dark wavy hair, the romantic type . . ."

"Sold," Gertie announced, and then added with a laugh, "and, I'll either crack that alibi of his or I'll prove that he has genuine amnesia. One or the other."

Mason said, "I'll bet you will! But first, detectives are watching the office. I want to ditch them once and for all, but I don't want them to know that I am trying to ditch them or they will realize we've got something important on.

"Here's what we'll do. We leave the office together. Downstairs in the lobby we stop and chat for a minute or so. Then I leave you two as though I were starting for court.

"You go into the department store across the street. I'll take the car, drive two blocks down the street and park in front of a fire plug. At this time of day cars will be parked solid everywhere else. Now, the shadows, if they're clever, will be following along behind. There will be two of them, one to stay in the automobile and the other to follow me in case I should leave my car. They won't be able to park anywhere near me, and they won't dare to double-park. That will take care of the car and the driver. He'll just have to keep going. The second man will have to jump out and follow me on foot. I won't try and ditch him at all. I'll go to the nearest telephone, call up Paul Drake, give him some instructions, leave the phone and start walking down the street as though, after my conversation with Drake, I'd thought of something else I had to do.

"You girls leave the department store, walk down the street and you'll find my automobile parked in front of a fire plug on the right-hand side two blocks down. I'll pick the first fire plug I can find. Della, you have the keys to my car. There'll probably be a parking tag on it. You may even find the cop in the act of putting on the tag and he'll start bawling you out. Don't pay any attention to that. Just get in and drive off. I'll go into the interurban station. My man will be following me, of course, but by that time his partner and his car will be out of the running. Now you synchronize your watches with mine. I'll take the first interurban car that leaves after an interval of

151

exactly twenty minutes to the second from the time I say good-by to you girls. I'll be back in the car in a seat on the right-hand side, next to the window. For all my shadow can tell, I'll be going all the way on the interurban.

"You girls drive on out Seventh Street, park the car at a point that's far enough out so that my shadow can't pick up a taxicab. You keep watch on the red interurban cars. I'll be watching for you. When my car passes, I'll signal you and you fall in behind the car. I'll ride out to a point that's sufficiently isolated, then get off. My shadow will, of course, be right behind me. But you'll be there with the car. I'll step into the automobile, and as I do so, I'll tell you all about exactly how many minutes it took me to go from the terminal to the point where I got off. The shadow will think I was making some sort of a test to check up on the story of a witness and he'll be left there twiddling his thumbs, hoping for a taxi, perhaps trying to stop some passing motorist and offer him five bucks to follow us.

"The whole thing will depend on split-second timing. We want to get away from there fast, before the shadow can make any possible connections with any kind of transportation, so be sure we have a smooth, steady, well-timed operation that goes like clockwork."

"And then?" Della Street asked.

Mason said, "Then you make the first turn off the main road and I'll tell you where to go from there. We'll wind up in Gertie's apartment. Gertie, you're inviting us to spend the day and to have dinner. We'll pick up some food at a delicatessen place, and wait up in your apartment."

Gertie said, "Gee that's swell. I just started one of those diets and I've counted calories until I feel like my belt buckle is scraping against my backbone. I've just been looking for a good excuse to throw the whole thing overboard, and I think this is it! You always did like tenderloin steaks, Mr. Mason, and my butcher said he'd been saving some for me. After all, when a girl changes from the status of an unattached female to a blushing bride, the occasion calls for *some* celebration."

# Chapter 12

It was seven-thirty. Out in Gertie's kitchenette the girls were busy doing the dishes. They had been cooped up in the place all day, playing cards, listening to the radio, phoning Paul Drake, dozing fitfully.

Perry Mason, sitting in one overstuffed chair which the apartment offered, chain smoked cigarettes and frowningly regarded the faded carpet. As Paul Drake had so aptly pointed out, it could well be a week before they found any trace of Bob Fleetwood.

The open window on the shaft gave a partial ventilation, sufficient to let in some air, but not enough to dispel the heavy odors of cooking, the aroma of broiled steaks, of coffee.

For the third time in ten minutes Mason glanced impatiently at his wrist watch.

Abruptly the telephone rang.

Mason jumped for the instrument, scooped the receiver off the hook, said, "Yes, hello."

Paul Drake's voice, keen-edged with excitement, said, "We've got him, Perry!"

"Got Fleetwood?"

"That's right!"

"Where?"

"He's holed up at a little farmhouse — a little mountain ranch actually within five miles of where the car went off the grade."

"Wait a minute! Della, grab a notebook and get these directions as I repeat them. Go ahead, Paul."

Drake said, "At the foot of the grade you'll see a sign on the right-hand side of the road that says, 'Fifty miles of mountain grades ahead. Be sure you have plenty of oil, water and gas.' Now you set your speedometer to zero at that sign."

"That's at the foot of the grade?" Mason asked.

"Right. It's just before you start climbing, about a hundred yards or so."

"Okay, I've got it. Then what?"

"You go exactly thirty-one and two-tenths miles from that sign," Drake said. "That puts you well up in the mountains over the first ridge down in an elevated valley. There's a stream running along in the valley, but it's narrow and steep and you wouldn't think there was any farming land within a hundred miles. But right at that point you'll notice a side road that turns off. You follow that and it brings you to a little general store and post office at exactly one and four-tenths miles from the place where you turn off.

"Now you go right past the post office and take the first road that turns off to the left. It's a rocky dirt road that looks as though it would pinch out within the first hundred yards. It doesn't. It keeps on going. It's a rough, twisting rocky road, but it climbs up a steep grade and brings you to a beautiful little elevated mountain plateau with some good ranch land, about ten or fifteen acres of fine mountain meadow. There are two little ranches up there. You want the first one. You'll be able to spot it from the name on the mailbox. The name is P. E. Overbrook. I don't think he has any idea about what's going on. There's no electric power of any sort on his place. He doesn't have a radio."

"Does he know Fleetwood? Is it a hide out?"

"I can't tell you that," Drake said. "All I know is that when my man stopped at the ranch he saw Fleetwood walking around the house. He only had Fleetwood's description, but he's pretty certain."

Mason repeated the names, distances and directions. "That right, Paul?"

"That's right."

"Okay," Mason said. "We're on our way. Are you in touch with your operative up there?"

"There's a telephone service at the general store, but I don't know how long you can get him there. And remember that up in that country it's all party line stuff. There'll be a lot of people listening."

"I know," Mason said. "If there should be any developments and you want to stop me, get someone up there to flag me down at the general store. We'll make time."

"Okay."

Mason hung up the phone, turned to Della Street and said, "You got those down, Della? All those directions and names?"

"I have them, Chief."

"Let's go."

156

Within fifteen seconds from the time the lawyer had hung up the telephone they were scrambling out of the apartment, Gertie still rubbing the last of the hand lotion on her hands.

Mason had taken the precaution to have his car filled with gas, and the machine, capable of road speeds in excess of ninety miles an hour, responded like a race horse as the lawyer struck the through-boulevard, crowding the speed limit, but keeping just under a rate which might result in a jail sentence.

Leaving the outskirts of the city, Mason stepped on the gas, and by nine-fifty had left Springfield behind and was climbing through the mountains.

Twenty minutes later, Della Street, who'd been watching the speedometer, said, "You're getting close, Chief."

Mason slowed the car, while Della Street watched for the turn-off.

Within a few minutes they had made the turn-off, gone over the dirt road past the post office, found the left-hand turn and were climbing over a narrow, rocky road that twisted and turned up a steep grade, then debouched onto a mountain plateau.

There was a barbed wire fence on one side of the road. The headlights illuminated the rich green of the pasture land. A hundred yards farther on the headlights were reflected from the aluminum paint on a mailbox. The name P. E. OVER-BROOK had been stenciled on the metal and Mason turned in on a short driveway.

The house was dark, and behind it a barn silhouetted itself against the stars. A dog started frenzied barking and the beam from the headlights reflected back in blazing points from the animal's eyes.

Mason shut off the motor.

There was no noise, save the barking of the dog, and after a moment, little crackling noises which came from under the hood as the cold night air of the mountains pressed against the heated automobile engine.

The dog ran up to the car, barking, circling, smelling of the tires, but not growling.

Mason said, "I think he's friendly," and opened the car door.

The dog came running up to walk stiff-legged behind the lawyer, smelling at his calves.

Mason called out, "Hello, anyone home?"

There was the flicker of a match, then after a moment, the reddish glow of an oil lamp.

"Hello! What is it?" a man's voice asked.

"A very important message for you," Mason said. "Open the door, will you?"

"All right. Wait a minute."

They could see a bulky shadow moving around the room. Then, after a moment, the brilliant glare of a gasoline lantern gave additional illumination. They heard steps in the house and the door opened.

Overbrook, a big sleepy giant of a man with a nightshirt tucked into the waistband of jeans, was standing in the doorway, holding a gasoline lantern.

"Okay, Gertie," Mason said in an undertone, "do your stuff."

Gertie pushed forward into the circle of illumination from the gasoline lantern.

"You're Mr. Overbrook?" she asked breathlessly.

"That's right, ma'am."

"Oh," Gertie said breathlessly, "I'm so glad! Tell me, do you have William here? Is he all right?"

"William?" Overbrook asked vacantly.

"Her husband," Mason interposed sympathetically.

The big rancher shook his head slowly.

"The man who lost his memory," Mason explained.

"Oh," Overbrook said. "Why, sure. You related to him?"

"He's my husband."

"How did you know where he was?"

"We've been tracing him, bit by bit," Gertie said. "Tell me, is he all right?"

Overbrook said, "This place don't look like much. It's just a bachelor's hangout, but you folks might as well come in. It's a bit chilly out there."

They filed into the little room in the front of the house.

"Where's William?" Gertie asked.

"He's out back here."

Overbrook opened a door. "Hey, buddy."

"Huh?" a man's voice said sleepily.

"Somebody here to see you. Come on out."

"I don't want to see anyone. I'm sleeping."

"You'll want to see these people," Overbrook said. "Come on. Excuse me just a minute, folks. I'll get him up. I guess he's sleeping pretty sound. He's had a hard day, I reckon."

They heard voices in the little room which adjoined the living room on the back.

Della Street said, in a low voice, "Is he apt to take a powder out of the back door, Chief?"

Mason said, "If he does, it'll be an admission of guilt. If I'm right, and he's faking, he'll play out this amnesia business."

The voices in the bedroom back of the living room abruptly ceased. They heard the sound of bare feet on the floor, then Overbrook was back in the room. "I don't know how you handle such things," he said. "Do you want to break it to him gently."

"You didn't tell him his wife was here?"

"No. Just told him some folks to see him."

"I think the way to do it," Mason said, "is to intensify the shock as much as possible. You see, amnesia is usually the result of mental unbalance. It's an attempt on the part of the mind to escape from something that the mind either can't cope with or doesn't want to cope with. It's a refuge. It's the means a man uses to close the door of his mind on something that may lead to insanity.

"Now then, since that's the case, the best treatment is a swift mental shock. We take this man

160

by surprise. Don't tell him who's here, or anything about it. Just tell him some people want to see him. How did he come here? Did someone bring him?"

Overbrook said, "He came staggering up to the door last night. The dog started barking, and I thought at first it was a skunk or something. Then the way the dog kept up, I knew it was a man. I looked out to see if there were any automobile lights, but there weren't, and — well, I'm sort of isolated up here so I loaded up the old shotgun and lit the gasoline lantern.

"This man came up to the door and knocked. I asked him who he was, and he told me he didn't know.

"Well, we talked back and forth for a few minutes, then I had the dog watch him while I frisked him to see if he had any weapons at all, but he didn't. He didn't have a thing in his pockets. Not a thing. Not even a handkerchief. There just wasn't a thing on him anywhere that would tell him who he was or anything about him."

"Too bad," Mason said.

"There was just one thing he did have," Overbrook went on, "and that was money. He's got a roll of bills that would choke a horse. Well, of course, I was a little suspicious, and then he told me his story. He said that he had certain little hazy memories, but he couldn't remember who he was, that he was just too tired to think, he just wanted to rest. He didn't want to answer any questions, he didn't want anyone to know he was

161

here. He said he'd be glad to help with cooking around the place, he'd pay me money, he'd do anything, but he just wanted to rest."

Mason nodded sympathetically. "The poor chap gets these fits every once in a while. The only thing is, they're of shorter duration each time. This is the third one he's had in the last eighteen months."

"Shell shock?" Overbrook asked.

"Shell shock."

The door from the bedroom opened. A man in his late twenties, staring vacantly, his face slack-mouthed in lassitude, looked around the room with complete disinterest. His eyes held no recognition.

He was a man of medium height, weighing not over a hundred and thirty pounds, with good features, dark eyes and a wealth of wavy, dark hair.

"William!" Gertie screamed, and ran toward him.

Fleetwood drew back a step.

"Oh, William, you poor, dear boy," Gertie sobbed, and flung her arms around him, holding him close to her.

Mason breathed a very audible sigh. "Thank heavens, it's William!" he said.

Overbrook grinned, like some big, overgrown Cupid, who had managed to bring a loving couple into each other's embrace.

"I don't suppose he had any baggage or any-thing," Mason said.

"Came here just like you see him now," Overbrook said. "I loaned him a razor and bought him a toothbrush."

"Come on, William," Mason said, going up and patting Fleetwood on the shoulder. "We're here to take you home."

"Home?" Fleetwood said suspiciously.

"Oh, William!" Gertie exclaimed. "Don't you know me? Tell me, William, don't you know me?"

"I've never seen you in my life," Fleetwood said with some conviction.

Mason laughed heartily. "How do you know, William?"

Fleetwood looked at Mason with the eyes of a trapped animal.

"Of course, he doesn't know," Gertie said. "The poor boy can't remember. Come, William, we're here to take you home. You gave us an awful shock this time."

"Where's home?"

"William!" Gertie exclaimed reproachfully, and then after a moment added, "Don't try to think of a thing. The doctor says that the thing to do is to get you home, get you around familiar surroundings and then let you rest. That familiar surroundings will do the trick."

Mason said to Overbrook, "How much do we owe you?"

"Not a cent! Not a cent!" Overbrook exclaimed heartily. "He wanted to pay me, but I told him I'd do the best I could for him."

Mason took a twenty dollar bill from his bill-fold. "Get yourself something," he said, "a little something that you can remember the occasion by, something that will be a tangible expression of our gratitude. Come on, William, are you ready to go?"

"Go?" Fleetwood said, drawing back. "Go where?"

"Home, of course," Gertie said. "Come on, darling. Just wait until I get you home."

Fleetwood said, "You aren't my wife. I'm not married."

Mason laughed heartily.

"No, I'm not," Fleetwood insisted.

"How do you know you're not?" Mason asked in the amused tone of one dealing with a child who has taken some absurdly illogical position.

"I just feel that I'm not," Fleetwood said.

"You won't feel that way long," Gertie promised, her voice husky with emotion.

Mason said with professional gravity, "I wouldn't try to bring his memory back right now, Mrs. Raymond. I'd try and lead up to it gradually. These things take time."

Fleetwood stood hesitant, trying to find some excuse by which he could refuse to go with these people, yet failing to hit upon any logical defense.

Mason shook hands with Overbrook. "It's a shame we had to disturb you," he said, "but you know how amnesia victims are. We didn't dare to wait until tomorrow morning. He might have got up at any time during the night, had no recollection of where he was, and started out into the night."

"Oh I remember being here, all right," Fleetwood said. "You can leave me here. I'll go back tomorrow."

Mason smiled indulgently. "How did you get here, William?" he asked.

"I walked."

"From where?"

"The highway."

"And how did you get to the highway? Did you ride with someone?"

"I hitched a ride."

"From where?" Mason asked.

Fleetwood met Mason's eyes with sudden, cold hostility.

"From where?" Mason repeated crisply. "Come on, William, from where?"

"I don't know," Fleetwood said doggedly.

"You see," Mason said to Overbrook, and then added, "I really shouldn't have done that, but I thought perhaps I could push his mind back to some point where he could begin to remember. Let's go, Gertie. Come on, William."

Mason took Fleetwood's right arm, Gertie his left. They started him for the door.

For a moment, Fleetwood hung back, then sullenly accompanied them.

"I don't *feel* you're my wife," he blurted to Gertie, as he hesitated for a moment on the front porch.

Gertie laughed nervously and said, "You didn't

last time, either, and then for a while you thought you were living in sin." She laughed hysterically. "You, after five years of married life! Come on, darling."

They trooped out to the automobile. The dog, having accepted them now as visitors who had been given the approval of his master, stood to one side, gently wagging his tail. Overbrook, in the doorway, beamed at them with a broad, good-natured smile.

Mason opened the door of the automobile.

Fleetwood hesitated.

Gertie gave him a swift push that sent him scrambling into the machine.

"Come on," Gertie said. "Don't think you're going to get away from me again. You poor darling."

Mason said to Della Street, "You'd better drive the car, Della," and climbed in the back seat with Gertie and Fleetwood.

Della Street turned the car, blatted the horn in three quick blasts by way of salute, waved at Overbrook, and started back along the dirt road.

"Just what do you folks want?" Fleetwood asked.

"We want you," Mason said.

"Well what right have you got to take me with you? I don't want to go with you. Let me out of the car!"

Mason said, "Why, William, do you want to leave your wife?"

"She isn't my wife!"

"How do you know she isn't?"

Gertie leaned over and kissed him affectionately. "Just wait, darling."

"Say, what *is* this?" Fleetwood asked.

Mason said, "Of course, there *could* be a mistake."

"I'll say there's a mistake!"

"In case you aren't William Raymond," Mason said, "then your name is Robert Gregg Fleetwood, and there are a few things the police want you to explain. Now tell me, William, do you think you're William Raymond, or do you think you're Robert Gregg Fleetwood?"

"I tell you I don't know who I am!"

"Well, we'll do the best we can to straighten you out," Mason said.

"Who is this Fleetwood?"

"Oh, just another man who disappeared, the victim of amnesia. The police are looking for him."

"Well, I'll tell you one thing. I'm not going to stay with you until I know who I am. I don't like the idea of this woman claiming I'm her husband."

"Do you think you're Fleetwood?"

"No."

"Then you must be William Raymond."

"You stop the car and let me out of here. I guess I have some rights."

Mason said, "Let's look at it this way. Either you're William Raymond or you're Fleetwood. Now if you think that you're being abused, we'll

167

take you right to police headquarters, and you can tell your story there. They'll have a psychiatrist who will do the best he can for you. They'll either hypnotize you or give you a good dose of scopolamine. That'll start you talking and make you tell the truth. The drug lulls the conscious mind into oblivion and is the same as a hypnosis. It makes the subconscious take over. You'll answer questions just as a person talking in his sleep will answer questions."

"I don't want to go to any police station," Fleetwood said, in sudden panic.

"Well, you're either going to a police station or going home with Gertie. Just make up your mind which."

Fleetwood said to Gertie, "Okay. This is a game two can play at. If you want to play married, it's okay by me. You're a nice looking dish at that."

Mason said, abruptly, "Did you murder Bertrand Allred, Fleetwood?"

"I don't know what you're talking about!"

"When did you last see Allred?"

"I don't know any Allred."

Mason said, suavely, "Now, this was *after* you had lost your memory, Fleetwood. Amnesia victims remember everything that happened after their initial loss of memory. In other words, you remember starting out with the woman who said she was your older sister and then you both took her car and drove off — and then you met her husband. Do you remember that?"

"I don't remember anything."

"Since when?"

"I don't have to answer your questions. Who are you, anyway?"

Mason said, "You'd have to answer police questions."

"Why do you keep calling me Fleetwood?"

"Because you're either Fleetwood, in which event you're going to police headquarters; or you're William Raymond, in which event you're going home. Now just who do you think you are?"

"I guess I'm William Raymond if this girl says so," Fleetwood said.

"I certainly should know my own husband," Gertie said in mock indignation.

"Now look," Fleetwood said, suddenly suspicious. "I'm not going through any marriage ceremonies with any woman and I'm not going to register anywhere with any woman as husband and wife. I'm not going to get trapped into any common law marriage, or anything of that sort!"

"Listen to him," Gertie said reproachfully. "He wants to get away from me. Why, darling, before we were married, you told me I was the only woman in the world for you, that . . ."

"For God's sake, *will* you shut up!" Fleetwood shouted.

"And then, of course," Mason went on suavely, "if you are Fleetwood, there's a man by the name of George Jerome who wants to talk with you, and another man named Keith, who is very anxious to get in touch with you. I could probably get myself a piece of change by delivering you to either one of them. Keith, in particular, is very anxious to get in touch with you. Nice fellow, Keith. Do you know him?"

"I don't know anyone!"

"Now, William, don't be difficult," Gertie said chidingly.

"God, but you get in my hair!" Fleetwood said.

"I'm being rebuffed," Gertie said archly, "and by my own husband. That wasn't the way you talked five years ago, that moonlit night on the lake, William."

Della Street reached the paved highway, turned back down the mountains, sent the car gliding smoothly along the curves.

"I could bust my way out of here, you know," Fleetwood said. "I don't see anyone who's going to stop me."

"Look again," Mason told him.

"This is kidnapping. You know what *that* means."

"It's not kidnapping. I've simply found a victim of amnesia. I'm taking him to police headquarters."

"Me? Police headquarters?"

"That's right."

"I don't want to go to police headquarters."

"If you want to make the situation entirely legal," Mason said, "that's the place for you."

"Who said anything about making it legal?"

"You didn't want to come with me of your own

free will," Mason said. "You called it kidnapping. You're mentally sick. You admit that you don't know who you are. Perhaps, after all, Gertie has made a mistake, and police headquarters is the best place for you."

"Suppose I remembered who I was? Then you'd have to turn me loose."

"Then," Mason admitted. "I'd have to turn you loose. Who are you, Fleetwood?"

Fleetwood hesitated for nearly ten seconds. "I don't know," he said at length.

"Well," Mason told him, "if you're William Raymond, you go with Gertie. If you're Robert Fleetwood, you go to police headquarters."

Fleetwood settled back in the cushions and said, "Okay, I go with Gertie. I guess it won't be so bad, after all. Give me a kiss, sweetheart."

"Not now," Gertie said, suddenly cold. "You've repulsed me in public. I don't know but what perhaps I'll get a divorce."

Fleetwood, suddenly beginning to enjoy the situation, said, "But I didn't know who you were then, darling."

"Do you now?"

"No, but I'm willing to take your word for it. I don't give a damn whether you love me or not. You're married to me."

"No," Gertie said, drawing away from him. "I've had a stroke of amnesia myself. I can't remember who you are. I think you're a stranger."

Fleetwood said, "The whole outfit is nuts. Let me out of here!"

171

Della kept driving smoothly.

Mason gave himself to silent smoking.

After a while Fleetwood said, "Who's this All-red you've been talking about?"

"I thought you might recognize the name."

"It sounds sort of familiar. Tell me more about him."

"What do you want to know about him?"

"Who was he?"

"What makes you think he's dead?"

"I didn't say he was dead."

"You asked who he *was*."

"Well, I don't know."

"But why didn't you say, 'Who *is* he?' "

"I don't know. Maybe you gave me the impression he was a dead relative or something."

"Do you think he's dead?"

"I don't know, I tell you! I don't know a thing in the world about him. Now shut up and stop cross-examining me!"

They drove for more than an hour, then Fleetwood, who had apparently decided on a course of action, said, "I don't want to go with you."

"Where do you want to go?"

"Home!"

"Where's your home?"

"I tell you I don't know, but I don't want to go with you. You are going to deliver me to this man you were talking about — what's his name — Dixon Keith? Yeah, I think that's it."

"You know Keith?"

"You mentioned his name. Where did you get

172

all this about a doctor saying that I needed to be kept quiet?"

"That's the standard treatment of victims of amnesia," Mason said.

They had another long period of silence, Fleetwood thinking in scowling concentration.

They entered the city. Della Street turned to look questioningly at Mason.

The lawyer nodded.

"Now the interesting part about amnesia," Mason went on, "is that when you do get your memory back and remember who you are, *if you have had genuine amnesia,* you won't be able to remember a thing that happened during the period you were suffering from amnesia. Remember that, Fleetwood."

"My name's not Fleetwood."

"Maybe it isn't," Mason admitted. "Anyway, remember one thing — when you get your memory back, and do know who you are, *if you have had a genuine amnesia,* you won't be able to recall anything that happened during the period when your mind was a blank. During your period of amnesia, you remember everything except who you are in your past life. Once the memory of your past life comes back to you, you can't recall anything about the interval of amnesia."

"Why are you giving me all that good advice?"

"Oh, I just want you to make a good job of all this," Mason said.

Della Street said over her shoulder, "How am I doing, Chief?"

"Keep crowding the signals," Mason said.

Della Street nodded.

From time to time she jockeyed the car through signals after the red light had flashed, but before oncoming traffic, which was not particularly heavy at that hour of the night, engulfed her.

The fourth time she did this there was the low wail of a siren, and a motorcycle officer said, "I guess you'd better pull in to the curb, Ma'am! What's your hurry?"

Mason rolled down the window on his side. "We're going to police headquarters, Officer," he said. "That's the hurry. If you'll escort us, we have a man to take there."

"No, you don't!" Fleetwood yelled. "You're not taking me any place. You . . . Let me out of here!"

The officer kicked the prop under his motorcycle as Della Street brought the car to a stop. Fleetwood struggled with the door, trying to get past Gertie.

The officer said, "Wait a minute, buddy. Let's take a look at this."

"No, you don't!" Fleetwood yelled. "You can't arrest me! I haven't done anything."

"What's this all about?" the officer asked.

"Police want this man," Mason said calmly, "for questioning in connection with the murder of Bertrand C. Allred."

Fleetwood jerked the door open.

"Hey, you!" the officer shouted. "Hold it!"

Fleetwood hesitated.

174

"Come on back here!" the officer said. "I don't mean maybe! Hold it. What is this?"

Mason said, "This man is Robert Gregg Fleetwood. He was the last man to see Bertrand Allred alive."

"Who are you?" the officer asked.

"I'm Perry Mason."

Fleetwood shouted, "*You're* Perry Mason!"

"That's right."

"Why, you dirty shyster!" Fleetwood shouted. "You've tricked me. You're Lola Allred's lawyer. I know all about you."

"And how did you know I was a lawyer?" Mason asked. "And how did you know that Mrs. Allred's first name is Lola?"

Fleetwood paused for a moment, took long breaths, and suddenly clapped his hand to his forehead, "I've got it now!"

"Got what?" the officer asked.

"The whole thing," Fleetwood said. "It all comes back to me! For a minute my mind was going around in circles and now I suddenly know who I am. I'm Robert Gregg Fleetwood!"

"And where have you been?" Mason asked.

"I can't remember," Fleetwood said. "The last thing I can remember is a rainy night. I was talking with Bertrand Allred and I started to go home to get dressed for dinner and something hit me. I can't remember a thing after that. My mind is a blank!"

Mason grinned at the officer, flashed him a broad wink, but his voice was sympathetic as he said, "Poor Fleetwood! He's subject to fits of amnesia. Now when we picked him up in the mountains, he didn't know who he was. He couldn't remember his name at all."

"It's come back to me now," Fleetwood said.

"And where have you been in the last two or three days?" Mason asked.

"I don't know," Fleetwood said. "I feel sick. I'm nauseated. My mind is a blank as far as the last few days are concerned."

Mason said to the officer, "You want to use the siren and clear the way to police headquarters? I think Lieutenant Tragg of the homicide squad wants to talk with this man."

The traffic officer said, "This is going to be a feather in my cap, Mason. I guess I owe you one for this. Come on, let's go! Can this girl follow the siren?"

"You get your siren going good and loud," Mason said, "and don't look behind you. She'll have the radiator pushed right up against the rear wheel of your motorcycle."

"Let's go!" the officer said.

Gertie slammed the car door shut. Fleetwood settled back into sullen silence, between Mason and Gertie.

The officer kicked on his red spotlight and the siren. Della Street threw the car into second gear and then after the second block, slammed it into high.

They screamed their way through the frozen night traffic of the city, until, within a matter of minutes, the officer flagged them to a stop in front of police headquarters.

He walked back to the car, said to Fleetwood, "Okay, buddy, you come with me!"

Fleetwood opened the door of the car, crowded past Mason.

"Right this way," the officer said to Fleetwood.

Fleetwood gave Mason a venomous look, turned and followed the officer.

# Chapter 13

Mason waited until the officer and Fleetwood had entered police headquarters, and then he, himself, entered the building and found a telephone booth, dialed the number of Paul Drake's office and said to Drake's night secretary, "Perry Mason talking. I have to get in touch with Paul immediately. Where can I locate him?"

"He's home, getting some shut-eye," she said.

"Okay. I'll call him there."

Mason hung up, dialed the number of Drake's apartment, and after a few moments heard Drake's voice, thick with sleep, on the wire.

"Wake up, Paul," Mason said. "We're in the middle of a mess!"

"Oh, Lord," Drake groaned. "I should have known it. You spend all day sleeping in Gertie's apartment, and then . . ."

"Sleeping, hell!" Mason interrupted. "Playing cards, trying to keep awake sitting in a chair, and dozing. A more unsatisfactory day's sleep I've never had!"

"All right, all right!" Drake said. "What's wrong now?"

"We got Fleetwood," Mason said. "I got him to police headquarters. He didn't know who I was. Then I suddenly sprung it on him in front of some witnesses. That trapped him. He started cussing me for being Mrs. Allred's lawyer, and then realized he'd trapped himself into a betrayal of the amnesia business. So he clapped his hand to his head and said his memory had come back with a rush."

"Good stuff!" Drake said.

"A lot depends on what happens in the next sixty minutes," Mason said. "Have you got someone you can use here at headquarters to . . ."

"That's easy," Drake said. "One of the men I use is accredited as a special correspondent and has the privileges of the pressroom. Unless there's quite a hush-hush . . ."

"Get him on the job quick," Mason said. "I'm going to need some co-operation. And get dressed and get up to your office, Paul. We're going to have to do something fast."

"How come?"

"I think this fellow, Fleetwood, may be half smart," Mason said, "and we may either win or lose this case, as far as my client is concerned, within the next sixty minutes."

"Okay," Drake said, "I'll get my man on the job and have him up there. Anything else?"

"That's all for now," Mason said. "Well, wait a minute! This rancher, Overbrook, looks like a big, good-natured, rugged individual, but I'd like to find out something about him."

"Didn't you talk with him, Perry?"

"Sure, but I couldn't talk with him the way I wanted to because of Fleetwood being there and because I had to pretend Fleetwood was Gertie's husband."

"I see. Okay, I'll try and get everything I can lined up. I'll start working on the telephone from here, and then I'll be up at the office in fifteen minutes."

"That's fine," Mason said. "I'll be seeing you there."

Mason left the phone booth, walked to the office of the homicide squad, said to the officer who was at the switchboard, "How about Lieutenant Tragg? Is he in?"

"Fortunately, he is," the man said. "A big break in the Allred case found Tragg in his office."

"Tell him Perry Mason wants to see him."

"He won't see anyone for a while. He's interviewing a witness and . . ."

"You get the word to him that Perry Mason is out here and wants to see him for about two minutes. Tell him it may make a difference in the way he questions Fleetwood."

"Okay, I'll tell him," the officer said, got up from the switchboard, and walked down to Tragg's private office.

A minute later he came out and said, "Stick around for a few minutes, Mr. Mason. Tragg will come out just as soon as he gets a chance."

Mason nodded, took a cigarette and settled back in one of the uncushioned oak chairs.

The cigarette was half gone when the door was pushed open explosively, and Lieutenant Tragg came bustling out.

180

"Hello, Mason. What's on your mind?"

Mason walked over, took Tragg's arm, led him to one corner of the room, said, "You're always telling me I don't co-operate. This is one you can put on the credit side of the ledger."

"Damned if it isn't!" Tragg said. "How did you find him?"

"I knew he was supposed to be suffering from amnesia."

"Okay. What's the rest of it?"

Mason said, "He didn't get his memory back until just before he entered headquarters."

"That's what the traffic officer was telling me."

Mason said, "As soon as he got his memory back, of course he forgot everything that had happened during the time he had amnesia. He remembers walking along a hedge in the Allred patio, and then something hit him, he went blooey, and he doesn't know a thing until he came to in front of headquarters."

"I'm wrestling with this amnesia business," Tragg said grimly, "and I think I'm going to cure it."

Mason said, "Perhaps I can help you on that. You see, we know pretty much what happened to him during the last two or three days."

"Okay, what was it?"

"There's a price for it."

"The hell there is!"

"That's right."

"What?"

"I want to see Mrs. Allred now."

"This is no time for visitors."

Mason said, "Phooey. In the first place, I'm her attorney, and in the second place, you haven't put her under formal arrest and charged her with anything. You've simply placed her where you can hold her."

Tragg said, "I should have known there was a catch in this thing somewhere."

"What the hell," Mason told him. "Do you want to look a gift horse in the mouth?"

"You're damn right, I do!" Tragg said. "Any time you give me a horse, I'm going to look in his mouth."

"All right," Mason said. "Go ahead and look in his mouth if you want to. All you'll find will be his teeth. He won't talk and tell you how old he is. Play it my way and the horse will do the talking."

"He might do the laughing," Tragg said suspiciously.

Mason shrugged his shoulders.

"What's going to happen after you see Mrs. Allred?"

"Then," Mason said, "she's going to make a statement to you. She's going to tell you her story, exactly what happened."

Tragg scribbled out a pass. "Okay, take this to the matron," he said.

"And you can phone her," Mason pointed out. "That will facilitate matters. They'll have Mrs. Allred all dressed and . . ."

"Okay, okay," Tragg said, but then added,

"she's going to have to talk, though. Remember that!"

"She'll talk," Mason said.

"When?"

"At eight o'clock in the morning."

"Not before?"

"Not before."

"Why the delay?"

"I want her to have her breakfast," Mason said. "It might give her ulcers to talk on an empty stomach."

"All right, how about your dope on Fleetwood?"

"I'll be back before you talk with Mrs. Allred, and I'll give you ammunition that'll crack his amnesia stall wide open."

"That's a promise?"

"That," Mason said grimly, "is a promise. He was with a rancher named Overbrook. He walked in and said he had no idea who he was. I'm going to give you a chance to bust that story wide open. I'll give you the ammunition. You can shoot it."

"Okay, I'll telephone the matron. Go on over and see Mrs. Allred."

Mason took the pass Lieutenant Tragg scribbled, and went over to the detention ward. After a ten minute wait, he was taken in to see Mrs. Allred, who had quite evidently been aroused from a sound sleep and had had no opportunity to put on her make-up.

"We've found Fleetwood," Mason said.

"Where?"

183

"A rancher by the name of Overbrook — does that name mean anything to you?"

She shook her head.

"Within five miles of the place where the car went off the grade," he said. "The story is that Fleetwood had walked up to Overbrook's house Monday night, suffering from amnesia. Any suggestions?"

She shook her head.

Mason said, "I want to give you one last chance to think over your story."

"What about it?"

"Is it the truth?"

"Yes."

Mason said, "Somehow, I think Fleetwood is going to try to hang one on you."

"How?"

"I don't know how," Mason said. "I do know that this amnesia business of his is just a gag. I trapped him into betraying himself just before I took him to police headquarters."

"Then he'll tell them everything?"

Mason shook his head. "He'll tell them everything up to the time he received a blow on the head. After that he doesn't know what happened. He can't remember."

"Are you sure?"

"Of course, I'm sure," Mason said. "He has to adopt that position because a victim of true amnesia can't remember anything that happened during his periods of amnesia."

"But does Fleetwood know that?"

"You're damn right he knows it," Mason said, and added with a grin, "I took particular pains to tell him."

"Oh, I see."

"Now then," Mason said, "here's the point. As long as we could have you keep quiet, Tragg didn't dare to go ahead and put a murder charge against you, or do too much talking for the newspapers — not on the evidence he had. He was afraid he might have to back up after he'd caught Fleetwood.

"Now then that situation is ended. I think Fleetwood's going to try to hang it on you. My strategy is to start hanging it on Fleetwood."

"What do you mean?"

Mason said with a grin, "I mean I'm going to pin it on him if I can."

"Why?"

"In order to save you."

"You mean you'd *frame* him for murder?"

Mason said, "I'll frame him until I get him in such a position that the heat proves too much for him, then he'll begin to start squirming. Understand, he's taken advantage of this amnesia business. He's hiding behind a wall of blank memory.

"That puts him in a particularly vulnerable position, because while he can't be questioned by the police about the things that happened *after* he was hit on the head, he naturally can't *deny* anything. Therefore, I can make even the wildest accusations against him, and he isn't in a position to deny them. He has to take them with a bowed head and the simple statement that he can't remember.

"I'm going to keep piling on the straws until I break the camel's back."

"But then suppose his story is — well, suppose by that time he's had a chance to think up a story that —"

"That's exactly it," Mason said. "I'm going to try and push him into something before he's had a chance to think up a story.

"Now, then, when he does crack, he's going to try to pin it on you. He'll swear to anything he has to. So far, there are just two people who could have killed your husband and put the body in *your* car. You are one and Fleetwood is the other.

"In a case of this sort, public sympathy is a big thing. If you refuse to make any statement after the police really and truly turn on the heat, that fact will be spread all over the pages of the newspapers and will be a suspicious circumstance that will alienate the sympathies of the newspaper readers.

"Tomorrow morning Tragg is going to interview you. You're going to talk with him freely and frankly. You're going to try and talk your way out of a murder rap. It isn't going to be easy. If you're telling the truth, you can do it. If you're not telling the truth, you'd better do a lot of revising . . ."

"I'm telling the truth, Mr. Mason."

"Then," Mason told her, "that's all there is to it."

"And I'm to talk to Lieutenant Tragg?"

"Sing like a skylark," Mason told her. "Bare your soul to him. Pose for pictures in the newspapers. Tell everybody everything. Have nothing to conceal. Only be sure that it's the truth, because if you try to lie, you'll get caught, and if they catch you in a lie it'll mean life imprisonment, perhaps the death penalty."

"What I told you is the truth, Mr. Mason."

"Okay. At eight o'clock tomorrow morning start broadcasting."

"And you think you can make Fleetwood talk before tomorrow morning?"

Mason said, "I'm going to be a busy little boy, and when I get done I'm going to put so much heat on Bob Fleetwood that the varnish will begin to crack."

"I think you're very, very nice, Mr. Mason," she said.

"You don't know the half of it," Mason said, grinning. "Incidentally, while it's all right for you to tell them about Patricia clipping the corner of the hedge, and about finding Fleetwood lying there unconscious, be careful to emphasize the fact that Patricia didn't think she had hit anyone."

"But doesn't that make it worse? In other words, shouldn't Pat have known it?"

"Sure, she should have known it. You don't think for a minute she hit him, do you?"

"Why, Mr. Mason . . . I . . . She must have!"

"Phooey!" Mason said. "Your husband planted

187

his car in such a position that Patricia would have to cut the corner of the hedge. Your husband was the one who discovered Fleetwood lying there."

Her eyes were wide with the sudden realization of what must have happened. "You mean then, that it was all a plant that . . ."

"Sure it was a plant," Mason said. "Your husband cracked Fleetwood on the head. He thought he'd killed him. He had a corpse to dispose of with a nice little head injury. The best way he could dispose of it was by letting Patricia think she'd hit him with her automobile, and letting her take the rap."

Mrs. Allred pressed her knuckles against her lips.

"Think it over," Mason said. "Don't emphasize it. Let Lieutenant Tragg uncover it, then it'll be *his* baby."

And Mason walked out, leaving her sitting there.

# Chapter 14

"Drake in?" Mason asked the night janitor who brought up the elevator.

"Yeah. He came in fifteen or twenty minutes ago. You fellows must be working on something hot."

Mason said, "Oh, we're just keeping out of mischief."

Drake kept switchboard operators on twenty-four hours a day, so Mason, opening the office door, jerked his thumb toward Drake's inner office and at the same time raised his eyebrows in silent interrogation.

The girl at the switchboard, busy taking a call, nodded and pointed.

Mason unlatched the gate from the narrow, cramped waiting room, walked down the long corridor and into Drake's office.

Drake was talking on the phone as Mason came in.

He motioned the lawyer to a seat, said into the telephone, "Okay, I got it. Now give me that address again.

"All right. No, stay on the job. Just keep an ear to the ground and see what you can find out. Telephone anything that looks important."

Drake hung up the phone and said, "Well, that's a break. I don't know how much of a break."

"What is it?" Mason asked.

"That's my man down there at headquarters in the pressroom."

"What's he found out?"

"The last reports say Fleetwood is still sticking to his amnesia story."

Mason said, "That's not a break. That's something I want to talk with you about, Paul. What else?"

"He went through the motions of just having regained his memory, and called his girl friend."

"Did your man get her number?"

"Her name, telephone number and address."

"What's her name?"

"Bernice Archer."

"Her name hasn't entered the case. What about her?"

"Oh, he just called her to tell her that he'd been suffering from a lapse of memory, that the police told him he'd been holed up at the ranch of a man named Overbrook, that he'd just regained his memory, and that under no circumstances was she to pay any attention to anything she might hear about him, until he had an opportunity to explain things to her."

"What sort of a conversation was it?" Mason asked. "Was it difficult, do you know?"

"How do you mean?"

"Was the girl throwing a fit?"

"No. Apparently it was just a routine conversation. He called her, talked to her and then hung up."

Mason frowned, then said, "That doesn't seem right, Paul."

"Why not?"

Mason said, "Suppose you're a guy's girl friend. Every one of your friends knows that he's going with you. Now all of a sudden, the fellow takes a run-out powder. Apparently he's run away with a married woman. You don't hear anything from him. Then out of a clear sky, he rings up and says, 'Listen, sweetheart, don't believe anything you hear about me. I've had a lapse of memory. I'll be up to see you as soon as I can.' Well, that just isn't right."

"You mean the girl friend would throw hysterics?"

"She'd probably raise hell. There would be tears and recriminations, and then she would wind up with the question, 'Well, do you love me? Well, tell me you love me. Well, tell me this other woman was nothing in your life.' You know, all that sort of stuff."

"Could be, all right," Drake said.

"Of course," Mason went on, "I'm having troubles of my own, Paul, and I'm looking for loopholes everywhere."

"What's happening?"

Mason said, "My client tells me a story that's probably okay. She swears it is. It's a story that *could* stand up, if it had just the right props, but it's a story that could fall down mighty easy."

"Well?"

"Now this man, Fleetwood," Mason said, "is

191

in a spot. He pulled this amnesia business, and I managed to get him into the hands of the police before he'd had an opportunity to do too much thinking about it. Right now, he's stuck with the murder of Bertrand Allred. He was the last man to see him alive, and he can't deny that he killed him, because he doesn't know anything at all that happened.

"Obviously, a man as shrewd as Fleetwood is not going to let himself be placed in that position without trying to do something about it. The only thing that he can do is to come out and admit that all this amnesia business was a stall, that he remembers everything."

"The minute he does that, he's put himself in a hell of a fix," Drake said.

"I know that," Mason said, "and that's the thing that I've been counting on as a prop to help hold up Mrs. Allred's story — but a great deal is going to depend on what he says when he starts telling the truth."

Drake shook his head. "If he took Mrs. Allred's car, then he was the last person to see her husband alive. If he gives a load of this amnesia business to the police, and through them to the newspaper boys, and finally weakens and says that he knew what was going on all the time, it doesn't make such a hell of a lot of difference *what* his story is. I think his best move is to sit tight on the amnesia, regardless of how much it hurts."

"It might be, at that," Mason said, "and we don't want him to do what's good for him. We want him

192

to do what's good for my client. We'll force his hand. I think that he'll start telling the truth about the amnesia, and when he does he'll tell a story that will have been carefully thought out."

"It'll have to be quite a story, Perry."

"Well, he may be just the boy who can think one up. I'd like to force his hand, Paul. I'd like to make him tell his story before he's ready to tell it. I want to make things so hot for him, he'll start squirming and twisting."

"How would you go about doing that?"

"I think the first place to start might be his girl friend."

"Want to go out there first thing in the morning, and . . ."

"Why not go out there now?"

Drake made a little shrugging gesture with his shoulders.

Mason said, "What is it? An apartment house, Paul?"

"Uh huh."

Mason said, "She's had a phone call from Fleetwood. She's awake. She's probably curious. Let's go out and have a talk with her."

"Okay by me," Drake said. "I just swigged about a gallon of coffee, and won't be able to sleep tonight, anyway. I thought you'd probably have enough stuff to keep me going all night."

"That's fine," Mason said. "We'll drive out in your car. You have the address?"

"Right."

"Let's go."

They left the office, entered Drake's car, and Mason immediately settled back against the cushions, put his head on the back of the front seat and closed his eyes.

"Tired?" Drake asked.

"I'm just trying to think," Mason told him. "This isn't an ordinary case where you don't know what happened or how it happened. This is a case where the District Attorney is going to have to prosecute one of two persons for murder. One or the other of those persons simply has to be guilty as the facts now stand. If my client is lying, she may be guilty. If she is, I'm simply going to represent her to the best of my ability and let it go at that, but if Fleetwood is guilty and he is trying to blame it on my client, I'm going to try and outwit him."

It was some fifteen minutes later that Drake eased his car to a stop in front of an apartment house. "This is the place," he said. "We'll probably have to drive a couple of blocks in order to find a parking space. It's pretty well cluttered up with automobiles."

Mason said, "Looks like a place across the street there. That's a fire plug."

"How about it?"

"Sure," Mason said, "provided you can park and still leave access to the plug in case there *should* be a fire."

"Don't worry about that," Drake told him. "In case there's a fire these boys get to the fire plug all right. It's kind of tough on your automobile, but they get there. I saw one car that had been left locked in front of a fire plug. There was a fire and the fire department just chopped a hole in both sides of the car, put the hose right on through and went to work. When the owner came back, he had a car with a tunnel chopped through it and tickets for overtime parking and tickets for parking in front of a fire plug."

"Probably cured him," Mason said. "Wait a minute, Paul. That man looks as though he's going to get in a car and drive away. If he has a parking place . . . there he is, unlocking that Dodge. Hey, Paul, drive on past, fast!"

Mason dropped down, out of sight.

"What's the matter?" Drake asked, speeding up.

"That fellow," Mason said, "is George Jerome, Allred's partner."

"Want to try to tail him?" Drake asked.

"Hell, no," Mason said. "It isn't where he's going that's important. It's where he's *been.*"

"You mean he's . . ."

"Sure," Mason said. "He's been calling on this girl friend of Fleetwood's. What did you say her name was?"

"Bernice Archer."

"Drive around the block," Mason said, "then come on back. Perhaps we can get in the parking place that Jerome had."

Drake said. "He's a big brute, isn't he?"

"Uh huh."

"A powerful man like that could pick a fellow

up and break him with his bare hands. I'd hate to get tangled with him in an alley on some dark night."

"We may have an opportunity to do that very thing before we get done," Mason said. "He's mixing in this case altogether too much to suit me."

"What does he want?"

"He *says* he wants to get Fleetwood's testimony nicely sewed up in order to protect him in a lawsuit."

Mason got back on the seat. Drake drove around the block, found that the parking place which had been vacated by Jerome's car was still available, and skillfully parked his car.

The doors of the apartment house were closed and locked at this hour of the night, but there was an electric callboard and buzzer system.

Drake ran his finger down the directory until he came to the card of Bernice Archer, then pressed the button opposite it.

"Suppose she'll use the speaking tube?" Drake asked. "If she does, what'll we tell her?"

"She'll probably buzz the door open," Mason said. "She'll think it's Jerome coming back."

They waited for a moment, then Drake pressed the button again.

The electric buzzer signified that the catch had been thrown back on the street door. Mason, who had been standing with his hand on the knob, pushed it open, said, "Okay, Paul, here we go."

196

The small lobby was dimly lit, but they could see a corridor and an oblong of bright light which indicated the location of the automatic elevator.

"Jerome left the elevator for us," Mason said.

They walked down the thinly carpeted corridor, entered the elevator, and Drake pressed the button.

The elevator rattled slowly upward.

"You do the talking," Drake asked, "or do you want me to?"

"You start in," Mason said. "Introduce yourself as a detective. Don't say whether you're police or private, unless she asks. Start asking her questions about Fleetwood, about when she heard from him last, and things of that sort. I'll chip in if she gives me an opening. Don't introduce me. She may think I'm another detective."

The automatic elevator stopped. The door slowly opened. Drake, sizing up the numbers on the apartments, said, "Okay, Perry, it's down here to the right."

Drake knocked at the door.

The woman who opened it was about twenty-five, a blonde with clear blue eyes and skin which needed but little make-up. The silk robe did not conceal much of a strikingly good figure.

There was a wallbed in the room which had been let down. The covers were rumpled and the pillow showed that it had been in recent use. The door to the closet was open, showing several dresses on hangers.

Drake, assuming a hard-boiled voice, said, "I'm Paul Drake. You may have heard of me. I'm a detective."

"May I see your credentials, please?" she asked very quietly.

Drake glanced dubiously at Perry Mason, then produced a billfold which he showed briefly, then snapped shut and started to return to his pocket.

"Just a moment," she said, *"please."* She calmly reached out for the billfold, studied the card, said, "Oh, I see. This is your license as a *private* detective."

"That's right."

"And the gentleman with you?" she asked.

Mason grinned. "I'm Mason."

"A detective?"

"No."

"May I ask what you are, then?"

"A lawyer."

"Oh," she said, and then after a moment, "you're *Perry* Mason?"

"That's right."

"Then you're Mrs. Allred's lawyer."

Mason, beginning to enjoy the situation thoroughly, said, "That's right."

"Won't you gentlemen please be seated?"

She indicated chairs for them, and went over herself to sit on the edge of the bed. The bottom part of the robe slid away from a smoothly stockinged leg. She was wearing street shoes.

"It is pretty late, isn't it?"

Mason laughed. "Our business is rather special."

"I suppose so."

"And," Mason said, "we knew that you had already been disturbed."

"How, may I ask?"

"Bob Fleetwood called you."

"Oh, yes."

"You received his call?"

"Yes."

"And what did he tell you?"

"Simply that he had recovered his memory. I'm glad to hear it."

"You knew then that he had lost his memory?"

"No."

"But he told you over the phone that he had been suffering from amnesia?"

"That's right."

Drake said, "How long have you known Bob Fleetwood, Miss Archer?"

"About six months."

"You're quite friendly?"

"I like him."

"He likes you?"

"I think so."

"You heard that he had run away with a married woman?"

"I understood he had disappeared."

"You heard that Mrs. Allred had gone with him?"

"No."

"You read the papers?"

"Yes."

"You read that police were interrogating Mrs. Allred?"

"I understood so."

"You didn't know that she was away with Bob Fleetwood?"

"I didn't think so. No."

"You knew that there was at least an intimation to that effect in the papers?"

"Yes."

"But you didn't believe he was with her?"

"No."

"Do you believe it now?"

"I don't know. I'd have to wait until I can talk with Bob."

"When do you expect to see him?"

"As soon as I *can* see him. Whenever it will be permitted. I understand he's being held as a material witness."

"Did you know that Bertrand Allred had been murdered?"

"I heard it over the radio."

"How much did Bob tell you when he telephoned you?"

"Merely that he was being detained, that he'd probably be detained for at least a day and that he'd had a spell of amnesia, that the police told him he had stayed with a man named Overbrook, but that he had recovered his memory and was feeling all right now."

"You were glad to hear that?"

"Naturally."

"It came as quite a surprise to you?"

"Not exactly. Bob has been subject to fits of amnesia before."

"Oh, he has?"

"Yes."

"You'd known about them?"

"He'd told me about them."

"Some time before this fit came on?"

"Yes."

Drake glanced at Mason and made a little shrugging gesture with his shoulders.

"You have an automobile?" Mason asked her abruptly.

She turned to regard Mason with the cautious appraisal of the fighter sizing up an adversary.

"Yes," she said, at length.

"Had it long?"

"Around six months."

Mason glanced at Drake.

Bernice Archer said, calmly, "I had it very shortly *before* I met Bob Fleetwood, if you're intending to put two and two together on the six months period of time, Mr. Mason."

"Not at all," Mason said. "I just noticed the fact that you had mentioned the interval of six months on two occasions."

"That's right."

Mason said abruptly, "Yesterday night, Monday, you took your automobile out, didn't you?"

She looked at him for some twenty seconds.

"Is it any of your business?"

"It might be."

"I don't see what that has to do with it."

"It depends on where you went."

"I drove out to the apartment of a girl I know, picked her up and drove her out here. She spent the night with me."

"Why did you do that?"

"What do you mean?"

"Did you think you might need an alibi?"

"Don't be silly! I wanted someone to talk to. So I got my friend and drove her over here. We talked until the small hours and then we went to sleep."

Mason said, "Bob Fleetwood is being a little foolish."

"Is he?"

"Yes."

"In what way?"

"I don't think this amnesia business is really doing him any good."

"What do you mean by that?"

"I mean he could have thought up something better."

"I'm afraid I don't understand you, Mr. Mason."

"Amnesia has come to be pretty much of a racket. It happens quite frequently that when a person wants to escape the responsibility for something, he says his mind was a blank."

"Have you talked with Bob?"

"Yes."

"Don't you believe he really had amnesia?"

"No."

"Then why should he pretend that he did?"

"It gets him out of rather an embarrassing situation."

"I'm afraid I don't understand."

"Telling what he knows about what happened to Bertrand Allred."

"He doesn't know anything about that."

"How do you know he doesn't?"

"I'm certain he doesn't."

"What course in telepathy did you take?" Mason asked.

She said, "I don't have to study telepathy to know what happened. Obviously Mrs. Allred killed her husband."

"And what makes you so certain?"

"I'm not exactly stupid, Mr. Mason. When you come out here and tell me what you think Bob should do, I know you're Mrs. Allred's lawyer. Therefore, what you want Bob to do is what you think would be for the best interests of Mrs. Allred, not for the best interests of Bob Fleetwood."

"Not necessarily. I try to protect my client's interests, but I still think Bob should throw this amnesia business overboard. He'll have to, sooner or later."

"And you came here hoping you could sell me on that idea, so I, in turn, would sell Bob on it. Is that right?"

"Only in part."

"My, my, what splendid consideration you show for a man who is almost a stranger to you, Mr. Mason. Running around at three o'clock in the morning, a high priced lawyer, getting me out of bed to tell me what Bob should do. It's touching!"

"Have it your way," Mason said.

"I intend to. And now let *me* tell *you* something."

"What?"

"Get rid of Mrs. Allred as a client. Let some other lawyer handle her case."

"Why?"

"Because you don't stand a chance, not a chance in the world."

"You think she murdered her husband?"

"I *know* she murdered her husband!"

"There's a motorist who can give her a perfect alibi. She hitchhiked a ride with him."

"Before or after her husband died?"

"Before."

"How do you *know?*"

"I know."

She laughed. "Because she told you so. That's the only way you have of knowing. And that's not good enough. Mr. Mason, I wish I could tell you what I know, but I don't think I should. I don't think the police would want me to, but I can tell you this much: Don't represent that woman. And now, if you'll excuse me, I want to go to bed and get some sleep."

Mason looked at the bed, and said, "You've

already been to bed."

"That's right."

"Do you always put on stockings and shoes when you answer the telephone?" Mason demanded.

She looked at Mason steadily without answering.

"You had another caller?"

"A caller, Mr. Mason?"

"Yes."

"I'm sorry, Mr. Mason, but I'm not accustomed to receiving people in my apartment at this hour."

"How about George Jerome?" Mason asked.

She looked at him with eyes that were suddenly hard and narrow. "Are you having my apartment shadowed?" she asked.

Mason said, "Before I answer that question, tell me whether you have been talking with George Jerome."

By way of answer, she walked over to the telephone, picked up the receiver, dialed Operator and said, "Get me police headquarters, please. This is an emergency."

A moment later she said, "I want to talk with someone who is in charge of the investigation of the murder of Bertrand C. Allred."

"Ask for Lieutenant Tragg," Mason interposed. "He's the one you want to talk with."

"Thank you, Mr. Mason," she said, and then into the telephone, "I think the officer I want is Lieutenant Tragg."

There was a moment of silence, then she said, "Hello, is this Lieutenant Tragg? I am Bernice Archer — that's right, the girl that Bob Fleetwood telephoned to a little while ago. I think I am a witness in the case. I have some information which may be of importance. There's a Mr. Mason, a lawyer, and a Mr. Drake, a detective — yes, that's right, Perry Mason — yes, it's Paul Drake — how's that? Yes, they're here in the apartment. Mr. Mason is very insistent that I should tell him what I know, and . . . thank you very much, Lieutenant, I just wanted to be sure. I thought that would be what you'd want me to do."

She hung up the phone, turned to Mason with a smile and said, "Lieutenant Tragg says to say absolutely nothing to anyone until I've talked with him, that I'm to come to police headquarters at once, and if you try to stay on here or interfere that he'll send an escort. And now, if you gentlemen will get out of here, I'll dress."

"Come on, Paul. Let's go."

"Mr. Mason, please do what I told you to. Please get rid of that woman as a client."

"Why?"

"Because she's guilty, and even *you* can't get her off."

Mason grinned. "You were sarcastic over my concern for Bob Fleetwood. You insisted on questioning my motives. Now I'll turn the tables. Your concern over getting me to drop my client — for my own good, of course — is touching

206

indeed. Do you suppose it could be that you're trying to cut your boy friend a piece of cake?"

She walked across the apartment, to the door. "Don't say I didn't warn you."

"I won't."

She held the door open for them. "Good night," she said sweetly.

They walked silently down the corridor. It wasn't until they were in the elevator that Mason said, glumly, "There's the brains of the outfit."

"Are you telling me!" Drake said. "Gosh, Perry. Think of a woman with looks like that and brains thrown in."

"Don't make any mistake about her, she's dynamite!" Mason admitted. "She knows that it has to be either her boy friend or Mrs. Allred, and she's playing ball with her boy friend.

"Jerome called on her. Jerome is mixed in this thing in some way that isn't apparent, as yet. All of these people are too damned anxious to get in touch with Fleetwood. Jerome undoubtedly posted her on everything the police know, to date."

"Providing Jerome knows," Drake said.

"I think he does," Mason said. "Anyhow, Paul, here's a job for you. Get hold of the telephone company, impress upon them how important it is. Get access to their records, look up and see if Bernice Archer's number that you got was called sometime Monday from Springfield, or from some of the service stations along that mountain highway."

"You think Fleetwood was in touch with her, Perry?"

"He must have been. Try the telephone company, inquire at the motel where they stayed. Cover the gasoline stations along that mountain highway. I'll bet ten to one that the phone call Fleetwood put in from the jail wasn't the first time he'd called her since he left. And if he'd called her before, I'll bet she's mixed up in this thing, right up to those delicately arched eyebrows of hers."

Drake groaned. "I knew you'd leave me with one of those rush jobs that are such a headache."

Mason grinned. "I try not to disappoint people. This will give you a preliminary warm up. A little later I expect to have a *real* job for you."

"Yeah?"

"Uh huh. I want you to reconstruct Bernice Archer's time from Saturday noon on. I want to know where she was every minute, what she was doing, and with whom she did it. Have you found out anything about Overbrook?"

"Just neighborhood reputation. He's a good egg, slow spoken, honest and poor. He mortgaged his property a year or so ago when he made an unfortunate investment, but he's a steady, hard worker and is getting the mortgage paid off. In the meantime, he won't spend a nickel for anything except his dog. He will buy food for the dog. He's tight as a shrunken collar. They say he hardly ever leaves the ranch and pinches every penny, even to the extent of buying stale bread."

"Any chance he knew Fleetwood?"

"Not a chance in ten million, Perry."

"Okay, Paul, keep plugging."

"On Overbrook?"

"No. The picture on him seems complete. Start working on that phone call to Bernice Archer. I'm betting ten to one such a call was made."

Drake opened his mouth in a great yawn. "I knew that sleep I had was just coincidental," he said.

# Chapter 15

It was shortly before six o'clock when the telephone in Mason's apartment rang a strident summons.

The lawyer, who had been dozing in the big easy chair, with the telephone on the table beside him, picked up the receiver, said hurriedly, "What have you found out?"

Paul Drake's voice came over the line.

"Well, we got another break, Perry."

"What?"

"We've traced a telephone to Donnybrook 6981, Bernice Archer's number. It was called on Monday night at about seven o'clock. The call was placed from a service station about five miles from Springfield. My men went out and interviewed the man who runs the station, a fellow by the name of Leighton, and he remembers the incident perfectly."

"Go on," Mason said excitedly. "What happened?"

"A car drove up and stopped at the gas pumps. A woman who answers the description of Mrs. Allred said she wanted the tank filled right up to the brim. There was a man in the car who answers Fleetwood's description. He seemed sunk in a sort of a lethargy. The way Leighton describes him, he was a lazy bump on a log who sat still and let the woman bustle around. He thought the guy was drunk at first and then came to the conclusion that he was just plain lazy.

"Then the woman went into the rest room, and the minute she got out of sight, Fleetwood came to life. He rushed out of the car, dashed into the service station, grabbed the public telephone, dropped a nickel, yelled for long distance, and called this number.

"The service station man remembers it particularly, because he got such a kick out of it. He thought that Mrs. Allred was the guy's wife, and that this fellow was trying to make a surreptitious date with his girl friend, or else explain why he had to break a date. The service station man didn't say anything, but kept on with the chores of filling the tank, checking the oil and water, washing off the windshield, scrubbing the windshield wings and all of that. It had been raining a little earlier in the afternoon and had settled down to a drizzle along in the evening.

"The man stood there waiting for his call to come through and watching the door of the women's rest room. Before the call was completed, the woman came out and the man dropped the receiver like it was a hot potato, ambled back to the car and settled down in the cushions with a look of utter vacancy on his face.

"The phone began to ring while the woman was paying for the gasoline. The attendant glanced at the man in the automobile, and the man all but imperceptibly shook his head. After

211

the car had driven away the attendant went over, picked up the receiver and answered the phone. The operator said that they were ready with Donnybrook 6981, that Miss Archer was on the line, and the service station man explained that the party who had placed the call had been unable to wait for it. There was some argument, the long distance operator claiming that the entire time consumed in getting the call had been less than four minutes. But the attendant said it didn't make any difference whether it had only been ten seconds, that the person who had placed the call was gone and what were they going to do about it."

"That was Monday night?" Mason asked.

"Monday night, a little after seven o'clock."

Mason said, "Okay, thanks! Don't go to bed yet, Paul; you may have work to do."

"Of course I'll have work to do," Drake said. "I'll have work to do tonight too. Have a heart, Perry. Give a guy a rest."

"You can rest in between cases," Mason said. "Stick around your office, Paul. I think I'm going to get some action."

Mason hung up the phone, then called police headquarters and asked for Lieutenant Tragg.

Tragg's voice sounded harsh and weary from loss of sleep. He answered Mason's call and said, "It isn't everyone I'd talk to at this hour. When do you give me that break you promised?"

"Right away. I'm coming up now. Wait for me."

"Hell, I've *been* waiting for you."

"Okay. You won't have to wait over fifteen minutes longer. I'll bust Fleetwood's amnesia wide open for you."

"Not that way," Tragg said. "You give me the ammunition and I'll do the shooting."

"This won't work that way," Mason said. "But I promised you I'd crack him and I will. Only I have to be the one that does it. If you try it, it'll be a bust."

"Well, come on up," Tragg said. "I'll be in the office waiting."

Mason said, "Okay, I'll be there in fifteen minutes."

Mason slipped on his coat and made time to police headquarters.

Tragg's office was impressive, the walls being decorated with display cases in which were knives, guns and blackjacks; below each of the weapons was appended a history of the case in which it had been used.

The furniture in the office told its own story of drama. The massive oak tables were charred along the edges where burning cigarettes had been placed while someone answered the phone, only to spring into immediate action at word of some homicide or attempted homicide, leaving the cigarette unnoticed to burn a deep groove into the table. Here and there were scratches and nicks where someone had thrown a captured gun or knife onto the table, or where some prisoner in desperation had beaten his handcuffed wrists against the wood.

"Well," Lieutenant Tragg said, "what's the score?"

Mason said, "Fleetwood is holding out evidence."

"You said that over the telephone."

"I'll prove it!"

"Go ahead."

"Get Fleetwood in here."

"He's going to be a witness for the prosecution."

"On what?"

"Well," Tragg said, "he . . ."

"Exactly," Mason said. "The man's memory is blank. He can't remember anything. Therefore he can't be a witness."

"He can be a witness to some preliminary matters."

"Yeah," Mason said sarcastically.

"Look here, Mason, if I get Fleetwood in here, and you start giving him the third-degree — well, suppose he gets on the witness stand later and you start throwing things up at him that he said at the time you were questioning him here, it's going to look like hell."

"For whom?"

"For me."

"Why?"

"Because I let you question a witness."

Mason said, "If your witness can't answer questions when you're here to see that I don't bullyrag him or browbeat him, he isn't going to make much of a witness when you put him on the stand

214

and I have a chance to pour the questions at him when nobody can stop me."

Tragg thought that over, said, "Okay, Mason. I'll get him in here, but I want one thing definitely understood."

"What's that?"

"I'm controlling the course of the examination. Any time I don't like your questions, I'll tell him not to answer them. Any time I think you're getting off the reservation, I'll have Fleetwood taken out, and I'll send you about your business."

Mason yawned, lit a cigarette, said, "What are we waiting for?"

Tragg picked up a phone on his desk and said, "Send that chap Fleetwood in here. I want to talk with him again."

A moment later a uniformed officer opened the door and pushed Fleetwood into the room.

"Hello, Fleetwood," Mason said.

Fleetwood looked at him. "You again!"

"Sit down," Tragg said. "We want to ask you a few questions."

"Who does?"

"Both of us."

"I want to sleep," Fleetwood said.

"So do all of us," Tragg announced gloomily. "But it doesn't look as though we're going to have much chance for a while."

Mason said to Fleetwood, "Bob, you got along all right with Bertrand Allred, didn't you?"

"Why sure."

"The thing that brought on your attack of amnesia was a blow on the head."

"That's right."

"How did it happen?"

"How do I know how it happened? I was walking along the hedge and all of a sudden, blooey, I was out like a light. The next thing I remember, I was riding in an automobile and you were talking about taking me to police headquarters. I have a confused recollection of things happening in between, but I don't know what they were. I haven't the faintest idea. That part of my existence is just a blank to me."

"You keep on saying it and you'll get so glib when you recite that formula that you'll sound like a needle stuck on a wax record."

Fleetwood looked at Tragg and said, "How does *he* get in on this? Does he have any right to sit here and pull that stuff?"

Tragg started to say something to Mason, but Mason said to Fleetwood, "You couldn't remember anything at all from the time that blow crashed down on your head until you recovered your memory here at the police station?"

"No!"

"Not a thing?"

"No, I tell you! How many times do I have to say that?"

"During that time you didn't know who you were?"

"No. Of course not. I was suffering from amnesia. I know what people have told me about what I did and what happened."

216

"Maybe you didn't talk to the right people," Mason said suavely. "Now there's a man by the name of Leighton, who is running a service station about five miles out of Springfield. He says that when Mrs. Allred stopped the car and got some gasoline and went to the rest room you darted over to the telephone and called Donnybrook 6981. In case you don't remember, or are having another attack of amnesia, Bob, that number is the telephone of Bernice Archer."

"Well, what's wrong with calling her up? She's my girl friend."

"I know," Mason said. "But how did you know she was your girl friend during the period that you were suffering from amnesia and didn't know who you were?"

Fleetwood started to say something, then changed his mind.

"And," Mason went on, "how did you know what her number was, if you couldn't remember anything about your past existence? How did you remember what her name was, and how did it happen that you knew that you must put through that call during the minute or two you had while Mrs. Allred was in the rest room?"

Tragg's chair squeaked as the lieutenant took his feet from the place where he had propped them on the edge of the wastebasket and sat suddenly upright in his chair. "What's this guy's name, Mason?"

"Leighton."

"Where is he?"

"Running a service station out there. Fleet-wood knows all about the place. Bob will tell you about it in a minute."

"I tell you I didn't know who I was and . . ."

"But you remembered your girl friend and remembered her telephone number!"

Fleetwood was silent, sullen under Mason's questioning.

"Now then," Mason said, "are you going to tell Lieutenant Tragg or am I going to bring Leighton in?"

"I didn't talk on any call," Fleetwood said to Tragg.

Mason grinned and said, "I thought all that part of your life was blank to you, Bob. Remember, that was during the time you were suffering from amnesia. How do you know you didn't talk on the call?"

"You go to hell!" Fleetwood shouted, jumping out of the chair. He swung his fist back for a haymaker.

Tragg's long arm shot across the desk, grabbed Fleetwood's shirt collar, slammed him back into the chair.

Mason had not even moved during the time that Fleetwood lunged at him and Tragg had pulled the prisoner back into the chair.

Now Mason calmly lit a cigarette with a steady hand, blew smoke at the ceiling, said, "There you are, Tragg. There's your murderer."

"What do you mean?" Fleetwood shouted. "You can't frame this on me. You're trying to protect *your* client, Lola Allred."

"Sure, I am," Mason said. "I'm trying to protect her by uncovering the real murderer. Here he is, Lieutenant. Here's a man who has consistently lied all the way through. He was the last man to see Bert Allred alive. Despite the fact that he tells you he got along all right with Bert Allred, he didn't. They'd had a big battle just before Fleetwood was knocked out. It wasn't any automobile that hit Fleetwood. He knows it and I know it! Now, then, you've caught him in a whole series of lies. First he says he didn't know anything at all about who he was, and he was lying. Now he says he doesn't remember anything about that."

Fleetwood glanced appealingly at Lieutenant Tragg. What he saw in Tragg's face was not reassuring.

"All right," Fleetwood blurted suddenly. "I'll tell you the truth, and the whole truth. Then you can see the spot I was in. Allred had a partner in some mining deals, a man named Jerome. Jerome was a pretty tough citizen. In working back over some of the books, I found where Allred had been gypping Jerome. Jerome wasn't the sort of a man you could gyp without having to face a lot of disagreeable consequences.

"I made the mistake of letting Allred find out what I had discovered. First he tried to bribe me to silence. Then he tried to threaten me to silence. Then, all of a sudden, he became very nice and suave and started telling me it was all a mistake

219

and that he'd explain it to me by producing some additional evidence, but that that could wait until tomorrow, that I could have dinner with them and that we'd forget about business for an evening.

"I pretended to fall for it like a ton of bricks, because I knew the man was desperate, and I was unarmed. All of a sudden I was afraid of what might happen. I just wanted to get out of there, so I told him I was going to change my clothes, and that I'd be back for dinner. I had managed to get George Jerome on the telephone earlier and told him who was talking, but Allred suddenly became suspicious and started back for the room where the phone was, and I had to hang up in a hurry and pretend I was rummaging around in the files. He finally came to the conclusion I hadn't phoned, but he was suspicious, and very edgy.

"Well, as I said, I started to get out of there, saying that I was going home to change my clothes, and he was all cordiality, patting me on the back and calling me his boy. It was a nasty, dark, rainy night. We'd been working until pretty late. I guess it was about half past seven or so. The Allreds have dinner at eight-fifteen every night. I left the wing of the house where Allred has his offices and started to walk across the patio, walking along the edge of that hedge. And believe me, I kept looking behind me. I was plenty jittery.

"I'd got to the point where the driveway comes in and had reached the end of the hedge when all of a sudden it felt as though fireworks had started going off inside my brain. Of course, I *may* have been hit by an automobile driven by Patricia Allred, but my own hunch is that Allred smacked me on the head with the blackjack, and probably hit me a couple of times more for luck while I was down.

"I know now what happened. Patricia was coming home in a hurry. Her mother was with her. They saw Allred's car parked so that the rear bumper was almost on the edge of the driveway and did the natural thing. They turned their car suddenly and a little too sharp. The fender on Pat's car went through the edge of the hedge. That was all Allred wanted. He thought he had committed the perfect crime. The only thing was, he hadn't taken note of the thickness of my skull.

"Later on he pretended to be very much concerned about Pat hitting me with the car. Patricia was half crazy with remorse. The minute I started regaining consciousness, I realized I was in a spot. At the time, to tell you the truth, I didn't know very much about Mrs. Allred. I didn't know how much she knew or whether she was in on what had been happening. I just knew that I was sick and hardly able to crawl and in the hands of people who wanted to kill me.

"So I got a bright idea. I pretended that I'd just regained consciousness. I had to. Allred was getting ready to load me in a car and take me to a hospital. I knew what that meant. So I opened my eyes. Then I put on the amnesia act.

221

"I think, at that, I fooled Allred. He wasn't *entirely* fooled but it would have been a beautiful way out for him. If I only had had real amnesia and couldn't remember who I was or anything about my associates, I wouldn't be in a position to tell Jerome anything. I wouldn't even remember what I had discovered about Allred's double crossing. And Allred would have a chance to get a deal with Jerome all closed up and be sitting pretty.

"Allred would have killed me if he'd had to, but he didn't want to unless he did have to. He told his wife that the thing to do was to take me some place where I could be quiet. She was to pretend she was my older sister and all that line of hooey."

Fleetwood turned to Mason suddenly and said, "Give me a cigarette."

Mason handed him a cigarette. Fleetwood lit it with a hand that was trembling so he had to steady the match with the other hand in order to get it to the end of the cigarette.

"Go ahead," Tragg said.

Fleetwood said, "Allred was smart. He sent me out with his wife that way, thinking that if I had genuine amnesia, he'd have time to do something about it. But just in case I was putting on an act he started spreading the word around that I'd eloped with her.

"You can see the beautiful position in which that put him. He could catch up with us, kill us both and claim it was the unwritten law.

222

"Well, Allred was pretending to be my brother-in-law, and I honestly thought that, if I kept up the amnesia act until he'd concluded a deal with Jerome, that would be all there'd be to it. But I hated Allred's two-timing, and I decided I'd get word to Jerome, if I had a chance, and tell Jerome to get a gun and come out and join us, have a showdown with Allred and take me away with him.

"Well, I never had a chance to get to a phone without getting caught; but I felt I had at least four or five days more. We left Springfield and drove a hundred miles or so north. Then Mrs. Allred got a chance to phone her husband. He evidently told her to come back and go to that Snug-Rest Auto Court.

"Well, we did it. We got to the Snug-Rest and waited there. We had a few drinks. Then Allred showed up. He told us to get our luggage together, because we had to move. Then when we were packed and had the luggage in the car, he suddenly told Lola to climb in the luggage compartment.

"I knew what was up right then. I guess he knew I was wise. He shoved a gun in my ribs, and when his wife tried to grab his arm, he socked her one right in the face. It gave her a bloody nose.

"Then at the point of the gun, he made her get in the luggage compartment. Then he slammed down the lid on the turtleback and told me to get in the car and start driving. I knew that he had me over a barrel. I drove the car. But, believe me, I was intending to drive it off the road and take a chance on a smashup. But Allred was wise. He wouldn't let me get up any speed. He said, 'Put it in low gear and keep it in low gear.'"

"What did you do?" Tragg asked.

"Well, you know how it is when you're driving a car in low gear. You have lots of control over the car and it's surprising what you can do to a passenger who isn't looking for surprises. We rounded a curve and I stepped on the throttle and the car shot ahead with all the power of the motor in low gear. Allred was thrown back against the cushions. He tried to brace himself, to push himself forward and push the gun forward so it would still be pointing at me; and then I slammed on the brakes.

"Stopping the car that way, right at the time Allred was pushing himself forward, slammed his body forward. His head hit against the windshield. I gave him an elbow on the face and the minute his head hit the windshield, I grabbed the gun and slammed the barrel down on his head hard.

"Allred went out like a light. He slumped down in the corner of the car over against the door on the right-hand side.

"I started to put him out of the car right then. But if I did that I was afraid he'd regain consciousness and tell some story to officers that would get me pinched for stealing the car. I just wanted to get away from Allred and wanted to get out of the whole mess. I decided to leave Allred in the car and get out and walk. However, I didn't want to do that until I was near a town or some place — and that's where I remembered this man Overbrook."

"What about Overbrook?" Tragg asked.

"I hadn't met him, but there had been some correspondence with him that I'd seen in the office. He and Allred had been in a mining deal and, I guess, Allred had trimmed him. But that's neither here nor there. I knew from the correspondence I'd seen that Overbrook had an isolated little ranch up in the mountains and that the road turned off within a few miles of where we had stopped. I got the idea of carrying on my pretense of amnesia. I knew that if it came to a showdown and I had to appeal for help, Overbrook would stand with me against Allred.

"Well, gentlemen, that was all there was to it. I came to the turn-off within a mile, took the dirt road, drove up to within a quarter of a mile of Overbrook's place, and swung off the road."

"What about Mrs. Allred?"

Fleetwood grinned and said, "Believe you me, Mrs. Allred had had all she wanted. She'd managed to work the catch on the inside of the lid of the luggage compartment, probably by using a jack handle. Anyway, she'd managed to get the lid unlatched. The minute I stopped the car, she raised the lid of the luggage compartment, jumped to the ground, and ran like a deer."

"What happened?"

"I called to her and said, 'It's all right, Lola.' "

"What did she do?"

"She kept right on going."

"Then what?" Mason asked. "Was Allred dead?"

"No, but he was still unconscious. He was breathing, a deep, heavy breathing. You could hear it all over the car as soon as the motor was stopped."

"You had Allred's gun?"

"Yes."

"Why were you so afraid of Allred? If you had the gun, why didn't you simply leave the car on the pavement, get out and start walking and . . .'"

"And where would I have walked?" Fleetwood asked. "It was a cold, misty night with a nasty drizzle. Everything was wet, and up in the mountains it was cold. I wanted a place to sleep and I didn't intend to be wandering around on the highway. And I didn't want to dump Allred out in the rain. I wanted to leave him the car so he could recover consciousness and drive himself home. I just wanted to get clean away from him, but I thought it would be swell under the circumstances if I could keep on with that amnesia gag. I had a girl friend, this Bernice Archer, and — well, I thought amnesia would be a pretty slick thing all the way along the line."

"Hadn't you been making a play for Patricia Faxon?" Mason asked.

"It depends on what you mean by a play. She is a pretty swell dish. I looked her over pretty carefully, and tried to find out if she wanted to play."

"Did she?"

"No."

"Didn't it go farther than that?"

Fleetwood said, "I'm no tin angel. I probably would have thrown Bernice Archer overboard and married Patricia if Patricia had given me the green light. I thought for a while she was going to do that, but she didn't. Patricia has dough of her own, and her mother is lousy with the stuff. The man who marries Pat Faxon doesn't need to worry about work, and if he knows a little something about mining investments, he can cut himself quite a piece of cake. However, that's neither here nor there. I'm giving it to you gentlemen straight. Bernice Archer was my girl. She still is. She's a sweet kid."

"You've seen her since you've been here?" Mason asked.

"Of course, I've seen her," Fleetwood said. "She came to me first thing when she knew I was here. She was with me for nearly an hour. She's a sweet kid."

"And did you tell her this story?" Mason asked.

"No," Fleetwood said. "I kept on with the amnesia gag. I thought it was the best way out of a lot of things."

"Did you fool her?"

"I don't know. You never can be too certain about Bernice that way. She pretended to be fooled."

"You didn't tell her anything at all about what had happened up there?"

"Certainly not. I told her I couldn't remember a thing that had happened from the time I was struck on the head there at Allred's house until I recovered consciousness just as I was being taken to the police station."

"All right," Tragg said impatiently, "never mind about your love affairs. Tell me the details of what happened. Mrs. Allred jumped out of the baggage compartment. Was the lid of the baggage compartment still up?"

"No. It slammed down when she jumped out. She didn't push it up far enough for it to remain in an upright position."

"And that blood in the baggage compartment?"

"The blood must have come from her bloody nose," Fleetwood said. "That's the only way I can account for it."

"So what did you do?"

"I'd got out of the car. I'd left Allred in it. Allred was still unconscious, but he was beginning to stir around a little bit and show signs of regaining consciousness.

"I knew I was within a short distance of Overbrook's house. I got out and listened. I could hear a dog barking and it sounded pretty close. I walked around the car and when I got in front of the car, I took the gun by the barrel and threw it just as far as I could throw it out into the darkness. I made a pretty good job of it. It seemed quite a while before I heard it hit the ground. Then I started walking toward the sound of the barking dog. I guess it was about three or four hundred yards before I came to the house. I knocked on the door. After a while Overbrook got up and wanted to know what I wanted. I told him that I guessed I'd been in an automobile accident or something because I found myself walking along the road with no idea of where I was or how I'd got there.

"Overbrook was a little suspicious. He looked me over pretty carefully. Finally he said he just had a bachelor's place there, that there was a spare room that had a cot in it, that it was just a cot and there were blankets on it but there were no sheets. He said that if I wanted to stay there that night, I could. I told him that would be fine, that I thought I'd have my memory back in the morning. I went into the bedroom and waited until he'd gone back to bed again. I had an idea of slipping out and listening to see when Allred regained consciousness and drove the car away. But I reckoned without the dog. Evidently Overbrook had told the dog to watch me, because when I tried to open the door a crack, the dog was standing right there in front of it with his lips curled back, and he gave a low growl.

"I went back and sat on the edge of the cot and I must have been there for about half an hour before I could hear the sound of a motor starting, and then the car drove away."

"What time did Allred get out to the Snug-

Rest?" Mason asked.

"You've got me," Fleetwood said. "Allred had previously taken, not only my watch, but everything I owned except my money. When I pretended that I was suffering from amnesia, Allred had been smart enough to see that I didn't have anything that would prove my identity in case I appealed to some stranger. I didn't have a watch. He'd even taken my handkerchief because it had a laundry mark on it, cleaned me out slick as a whistle."

"But he didn't take your money?"

"Not only did he not take my money, but I think he must have put at least a couple of hundred dollars more in the roll of bills I was carrying in my trouser pocket. He wanted me to have lots of money and nothing else."

Mason looked at Tragg.

Tragg shrugged his shoulders.

"How about Mrs. Allred's suitcase?" Mason asked.

"What about it?"

"When she packed up at her husband's request, she put this suitcase in the car?"

"Yes."

"And," the lawyer said sarcastically, "when she jumped out of that luggage compartment and started running for her life, do you want us to believe she was lugging this suitcase?"

"No, she wasn't, Mr. Mason. She was carrying a jack handle, or some metal rod; that's all. I could see that jack handle in her hand. The light

230

from the tail light showed me that."

The lawyer smiled triumphantly. "When the car was found, her suitcase wasn't in it."

Fleetwood's face showed dismay. "The hell it wasn't! Of course, I couldn't see her too clearly."

Mason said scornfully, "It's a hell of a story. She's in danger of her life, yet she comes back for her suitcase."

"Wait a minute," Fleetwood said. "I'll tell you what must have happened. Mrs. Allred was trying to hitchhike back to town. Allred recovered consciousness, knew I'd given him the slip. He started to drive back to town. He met his wife on the road. She may even have tried to thumb a ride, not knowing who was back of the headlights. When he stopped the car and tried to force her to get in, she hit him with the jack handle. It was then she got her suitcase out of the car and drove it over the grade. He must have overtaken her right about at the place where the car went over the grade."

"Bosh!" Mason said.

"Believe me," Fleetwood said fervently, "Allred got what was coming to him, and if Mrs. Allred ran that car over a bluff, she certainly was acting in self-defense. I'll bet if you get her to tell the truth, you'll find that her husband picked her up, that he tried to manhandle her and she cracked him over the head with a jack handle. She . . ."

The phone on Tragg's desk rang.

Tragg hesitated a moment, then picked up the receiver, said, "Yes . . . who? Oh, yes, hello, sheriff . . . that's right. I've just got a new angle on it . . . okay, go ahead . . ."

Tragg held the phone to his ear for some twenty seconds, listening attentively. He frowned thoughtfully at Fleetwood while he was listening. Then he said into the mouthpiece, "I wish you'd take a look at them yourself, sheriff, and I want to go along. It may be important . . . I can start in ten minutes . . . I think we've got something there. I think this business is all beginning to fit into the component parts of a perfect picture . . . Okay, I'll be over. I want to ask a few questions and then I'll get in touch with you. You be all ready to go, will you . . . Okay, good-by."

Tragg hung up the phone, regarded Fleetwood thoughtfully for a few seconds.

"Where did you stop this car?" he asked.

"I told you, about a quarter of a mile from Overbrook's house."

"I know, but what sort of a place was it?"

"Well," Fleetwood said, "it was not too good a place. It looked all right from all I could see driving along with the headlights. It was a nice level place off the road. But when I got into it I found the going was pretty soft. It wasn't so bad at first, but up where I left the car, it was fairly soft."

Tragg said, "Now look, Fleetwood, you've played tag with us long enough. This is the second or third time you've changed your story. Now, if you try to cut any corners on me, I'm going to throw the book at you."

"I'm clean now," Fleetwood said. "This is it, Lieutenant."

"I hope it is. Now you say Mrs. Allred jumped out of the car and ran?"

"That's right."

"Did she come back?"

"Come back!" Fleetwood said, and laughed. "You couldn't have dragged her back to that car with a block and tackle."

"You're certain?"

"Yes, of course. She was afraid of her husband, and she had reason to be."

"Did she know her husband was unconscious when she was running away?"

"I called to her," Fleetwood said, "but she kept on running."

"What did you say?"

"I don't know. I told her to come on back. And then I yelled and said, 'I've got his gun and he's lying unconscious here in the car.'"

"What did she do?"

"I *think* she kept on running. But by that time, she'd gone far enough so I couldn't see. Remember, she was running from the rear of the car, away from the illumination of the headlights."

"Where were you?"

"I'd just started to walk around the car. I was standing right close to the headlights."

"Then she could see you in the illumination of the headlights?"

Fleetwood thought a minute, then said, "Yes. Certainly, of course she could. I was standing right in front of the headlights. From where she was standing, she could see me clearly."

"So you don't *know* that she kept on running after you called to her?"

"No, to tell you the truth, I don't. The night was dark. There was a cold drizzle falling and you couldn't much more than see your hand in front of your face. I had quite a time stumbling along getting to Overbrook's house. I couldn't see a thing. All I could do was walk toward the sound of the barking dog."

Tragg nodded. "I have a hunch you're doing all right for yourself, Fleetwood. But you're going to have to remain in custody for two or three hours."

"It suits me," Fleetwood said. "I'm clean now. And believe me, Lieutenant, it's a load off my mind."

"You're sure you threw that gun away?"

"You're damn right I threw it away. You can check on my story if you want, Lieutenant. You can find the place where I left the car, and you certainly should be able to find the gun. I threw it ahead of the car and to the left, and it must have gone about — well, a hundred to a hundred and fifty feet. That ground was soft and I must have left tracks there."

"The tracks have been discovered," Tragg said drily. "I'm going up to take a look at them. They tend to corroborate your story a hundred percent. Now think carefully. You shut off the ignition on the car when you stopped it?"

"That's right."

"Did you switch out the headlights?"

"No, I left the headlights on."

"So the position of the car could be seen quite clearly?"

"Yes."

"And when you walked around the car, you walked in front of the car?"

"That's right."

"Where were you when you threw the gun away?"

"Standing right in front of the car."

"So the headlights were on you, is that right?"

"Yes."

"So anyone who was standing some distance back of the car could watch and see plainly what you had done?"

"Yes."

Tragg looked speculatively at Mason. "Your client tell you anything about this?"

Mason hesitated a moment, then shook his head.

"She should have," Tragg said.

"What do you mean?" Mason asked.

Tragg said, "Now I can begin to put the whole thing together. Your client ran down to the roadway, Mason. She stopped there. She heard what Fleetwood said about her husband being in the car and being unconscious. She waited. She watched Fleetwood walk around the front of the car and stand in front of the headlights. She saw him throw the gun away. Then she saw him start toward Overbrook's house. She waited. She had a jack handle in her hand. She knew her husband intended to kill her. She stood there in the drizzle, and in the darkness, waiting. When she saw Fleetwood didn't intend to come back, she tiptoed back to the car to make sure what Fleetwood said was correct. She found out it was correct. Her husband was just regaining consciousness.

"Mrs. Allred opened the car door on the left-hand side. She got in and proceeded to club her husband to death with the jack handle. Then she backed the car around, drove it back to the highway, down to a place where there was a sheer drop, took her suitcase out, threw the jack handle away, got back in the car and headed it toward the cliff, jumped out, leaving her husband inside, stopped a passing motorist and hitchhiked to town. Now then, if she wants to co-operate, she can cop a plea of manslaughter."

Mason said, "She didn't do anything of the sort."

Tragg smiled knowingly. "The tracks say she did, and tracks don't lie."

Mason said, "Fleetwood, if your story's true, how did it happen that you didn't . . ."

Tragg suddenly got to his feet. "I think that will do, Mason."

"How's that?" the lawyer asked.

Tragg was smiling. "You've done me quite a favor, Mason," he said. "You've got this witness to quit stalling around. He's told a story now that checks absolutely with the facts. And right now I don't want you to do anything to spoil it. You'll have an opportunity to cross-examine this witness when he gets on the witness stand. We can dispense with any further questions from you. You're going home and get some sleep."

Mason said, "There are just a couple of questions I want to ask, Tragg. A couple of points I want to clear up."

Tragg smiled and shook his head.

Mason said, "Hang it, I developed this whole thing for you. I . . ."

Tragg turned to Fleetwood and said, "No matter what Mason says, Fleetwood, don't say another word as long as he's in the room. Do you understand?"

Fleetwood nodded.

Mason, recognizing defeat, pinched out the end of his cigarette, said to Tragg, "Well, it was nice while it lasted."

Tragg grinned. "This is once," he said, "that not only does Perry Mason's client have her neck in the noose, but the great Perry Mason put it there."

"That's all right," Mason said grimly. "What I wanted was the truth. I knew that Fleetwood was lying about that amnesia."

"Who didn't?" Tragg said. "I was waiting for him to crack at the proper moment. But when you showed up here, I thought that perhaps you could soften him up for me. I didn't realize that you were going to play into my hands this far."

"I didn't either," Mason said grimly, and stalked out of the room.

# Chapter 16

The clock on the wall of the visitors' room of the county jail said that it was ten minutes past nine in the morning. Mason sat on one side of the heavy steel mesh which separated the two ends of the room. Mrs. Allred sat on the other side. At the far corner a matron waited for the lawyer to finish his visit with his client.

"What did you tell Lieutenant Tragg?" Mason asked her.

"Not a thing. He never came near me."

"That's bad," Mason conceded.

"Why is it bad?"

Mason sketched out Fleetwood's story, while Mrs. Allred listened intently. When he finished, there was a few moments silence.

Then Mrs. Allred said quickly, "It's all a complete lie, Mr. Mason."

Mason shook his head. "Something corroborates Fleetwood's story. I don't know yet what it is. If Tragg hasn't been hot after you for a statement, it means Fleetwood's story gets a good corroboration, all the way along the line. There are tracks, for one thing. There is only one explanation. You haven't been telling me the truth.

"Fleetwood stalled around long enough with one thing and another, but when he finally came

238

through with the story, he came through with a humdinger. It's a story that puts you in the position of committing a nice little murder. And the nice part of it is that provocation is there. And motivation is there. The thing is so marvelously tailored that the jury will sympathize with you, but will decide that you're technically guilty, probably of manslaughter."

She said, "Fleetwood must have killed him, Mr. Mason."

The lawyer shook his head. "I'm not so certain," he said.

"But he must have! It had to be either Bob Fleetwood or me."

"So it would seem."

"And I know that I didn't kill him!"

Mason said, "I wish that I could find some way of making a jury share your conviction."

"Do you feel that — that I'm in a spot?"

"Fleetwood's story," Mason said, "is one that sounds convincing."

"Even to you?"

Mason said, "I make it a point in my business to believe my clients always."

"If I weren't your client, Bob Fleetwood's story would convince you?"

"It might," Mason admitted. "I wanted to see what you had to say about having been in the luggage compartment of that car."

"I never was."

"Do you know of anyone who was?"

"No."

"There's blood on the carpet. The officers found that."

"So I understand."

"And you can't explain that? You didn't have a bloody nose?"

"No."

Mason said thoughtfully, "You know, if it had only occurred to you to tell the story that Fleetwood told, but dress it up with a few variations, it might have accounted for everything, including the blood on the carpet of the luggage compartment."

"But I told you the truth, Mr. Mason."

"There are times," Mason said, "when an artistic lie can crowd the truth right off the stage. The interesting thing is that Fleetwood's story is so beautifully logical and puts you in such a sympathetic light in front of the public. But it also hangs the technical killing of your husband right around your neck. I wish you could find some way of accounting for how blood got on the carpet of the luggage compartment."

"Well, I can't."

"That's the nice part of Fleetwood's story," Mason said. "It accounts for everything. It gives the police a beautiful, beautiful case."

"Against me?"

Mason nodded.

"I didn't kill my husband, Mr. Mason."

"Well," Mason said, "you've got to talk. It's got to a point now where it's your story against Bob Fleetwood's. Your story can't explain certain things. Fleetwood's does. There's some evidence I don't know about. Tragg's out investigating it now. If that evidence corroborates Fleetwood's story the way it would seem to, the killing is wrapped around your neck. I can get you off with manslaughter, or I *might* get a self-defense acquittal, but the responsibility for the fatal blow is yours."

"What evidence is there that could possibly give such corroboration?"

"Tracks for one thing."

"Well, my story is the truth."

"I hope it is," Mason said and signaled to the matron that the interview was over.

# Chapter 17

It was shortly before noon. Drake tapped his code knock on the panels of Mason's exit door.

Della Street opened the door.

Drake came in, followed by a thin man in the late fifties.

"You remember Bert Humphreys," Drake said. "He worked on that Melrose murder case for you, Perry."

Mason nodded, said, "Hello, Humphreys."

Humphreys nodded, the swift, competent nod of a man who has important information to impart and wants to get on with it.

"Sit down," Drake said to Humphreys, "and tell 'em your story." Drake turned to Mason and said parenthetically, "As soon as I got your call this morning saying to get a man up to Overbrook's place to look for the tracks of a car in soft soil, I telephoned Humphreys. Humphreys was working on the case at Springfield. He jumped in his car and beat it up there. He had at least an hour's start on the officers. He managed to get a complete diagram of everything that was up there before the officers arrived. They were sore as hell at finding him there, but there was nothing they could do about it."

"Go ahead," Mason said to Humphreys. "What was it? What did you find?"

Humphreys took a sheet of paper from his pocket, unfolded it, said, "I made a map. But, before I show you the map, Mr. Mason, I'd better tell you generally what happened. I got up to Overbrook's place and told him I'd come to investigate the car tracks. He thought I was from the sheriff's office and he spilled the whole thing to me."

"What did he say?"

"Well, it seemed that the more Overbrook thought things over about Fleetwood, the more uneasy he became. He felt certain from the way his dog had been barking that there had been noises before Fleetwood came walking up the road. And Overbrook came to the conclusion they might have been noises made by a car and by people talking when Fleetwood got out. So Overbrook, who's something of a hunter and tracker, started back-tracking Fleetwood."

"He could find Fleetwood's tracks?"

"Yes. Not right near the house, but reasonably close to it. You see, it had been raining hard Saturday and the ground was soft, and it's kept on drizzling more or less ever since, so the ground has stayed pretty soft. That gave Overbrook excellent tracking conditions."

"What did he do?"

"He back-tracked Fleetwood without any great amount of trouble, and came to a place where an automobile had been parked. Overbrook started to look the tracks over, and then he saw some things that made him do a lot of thinking. So he

243

didn't even stop. He kept right on going."

"You're certain of that?"

"Hell, yes. You can see his tracks plain as day. He walked right up to the spot where this car had been parked, turned in toward the place where the front of the car had been, then swung out in a turn and kept right on walking until he came to a farm road that was on hard soil. Then he walked back to his house, picked up a tractor and trailer, loaded the trailer with scrap lumber that he'd had hanging around ever since he tore down the chicken house, drove the tractor and trailer back to the place on the farm road where he'd come in, took the boards one at a time, and made a little boardwalk running alongside his tracks and right out to the place where the tracks of the automobile were located. He was particularly careful in laying the boards. He'd lay one or two boards, then walk back along the boardwalk to get more boards, come out and lay them, and walk back along the boardwalk again. In that way, he preserved every track there was in the ground. You can see the whole story there just as plain as day. He's a good, careful man and I guess he made a lot better job of preserving those tracks than the officers would have done if he'd left it to them. The way things are now, even with the officers milling around there, you can still see the tracks — or you could when I left. They were getting ready to use some plaster of Paris then."

"Then what?"

"After Overbrook fixed the boards, he drove to

the post office and telephoned the sheriff. He told the sheriff what he'd found and what he'd done, and the sheriff telephoned Tragg. They told Overbrook to go back and guard the place until detectives showed up.

"Well, I came out there and started looking around. Overbrook thought I was from the sheriff's office. He yelled at me to go around by the house and drive out on the farm road. I did that, and he showed me the boardwalk he'd built leading out to where the car had been parked, and told me what he'd found. I sketched the whole business, and had just finished my sketch when the sheriff and Lieutenant Tragg showed up. They were a little peeved about the whole thing, but thanks to the way Overbrook had laid the boards down, I hadn't messed things up any at all, and they couldn't make any real beef. Of course, they kicked me off the place and probably would have taken my sketch away from me if they'd known I had it. But Overbrook didn't say anything about it until after I'd got started. By that time, I guess the officers had troubles of their own. They were making sketches of their own and taking photographs."

"Let's take a look at the sketch," Mason said.

Humphreys spread the sketch on Mason's desk.

"Now here," he said, "you have everything. Here's the place where the machine turned off the road."

"Any question about it being the right machine?" Mason asked.

"Apparently not. Where the car was standing the ground was pretty soft, but where one car turned off the road, you could see the tracks of all four tires just as plain as day. Mrs. Allred's car had new tires on the wheels, and there were three different makes of tires. Because the car was making a turn, there's a place where the tracks of each one of the tires is distinctly outlined, just as though they'd been inked and then driven over a piece of paper. You can see every detail of the tread just as plain as day.

"I'd previously sketched the treads of each one of the tires of Mrs. Allred's car after the police located it down there at the bottom of the cliff. It's Mrs. Allred's car all right, or else it's a car that was equipped with absolutely identical tires."

Mason nodded. "I just wanted to clear that point up."

"Well, here you are," Humphreys said, indicating the diagram. "The road runs right along the edge of the tillable ground. On this side is a fence and alfalfa. On this side it's all open land and unfenced. Where the car turned off, the ground is soft. You can see tracks just as plain as you could in fresh snow. Now look at this sketch. Here's where the car turned off the road. It went up here and stopped. You can see where Fleetwood got out of the car. Here are his tracks where he got out of the door on the left side. You see, he walked right around toward the front of the car and across the headlights. His tracks show that he turned slightly when he got to this point almost directly in front of the headlights. He stood there for a second. First his footprints are in this direction. That's where he stood when he called out to Mrs. Allred when she jumped out of the luggage compartment of the automobile."

"You can see *her* tracks?"

"Here they are on this diagram. She jumped out of the luggage compartment. That's right where the luggage compartment would be located. Right there. She hit the ground and started running. You can see she was going just as fast as she could leg it, straight for this road. There's a graveled surface on the road so we can't pick up her tracks any more after she got to the road. But she couldn't have gone very far. She must have stood there waiting. It was right about that time, the way I get Fleetwood's story from listening to what the officers said before they kicked me off the job, that Fleetwood called to her that her husband was out like a light and everything was all right."

Mason nodded.

"Now then, you can see her tracks just as plain as day. She went down to the road, walked down the road some distance — no one knows just how far, probably never went out of earshot or out of sight of the car. She was thinking things over. She turned around and came back. Here are her tracks where she came back and you can see them heading just as straight as a string for the place

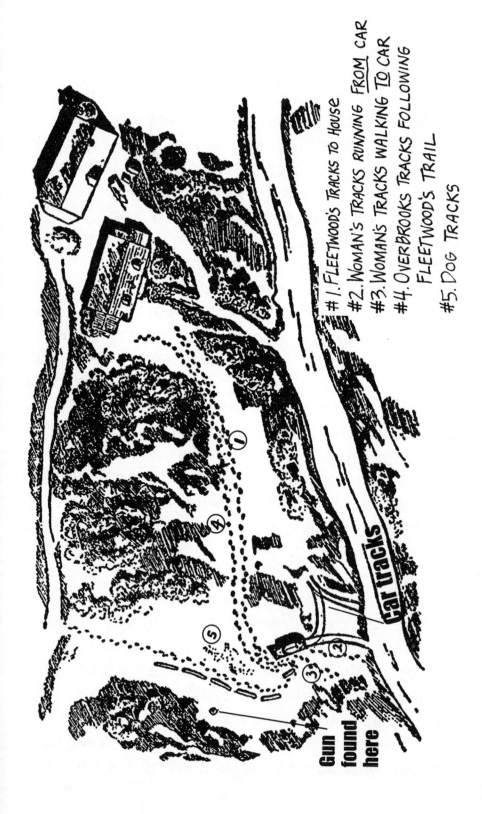

#1. FLEETWOOD'S TRACKS TO HOUSE

#2. WOMAN'S TRACKS RUNNING FROM CAR

#3. WOMAN'S TRACKS WALKING TO CAR

#4. OVERBROOK'S TRACKS FOLLOWING FLEETWOOD'S TRAIL

#5. DOG TRACKS

Car tracks

Gun found here

where the car had been left. She was headed right toward the left-hand door on the car — the driver's seat."

"Then what happened?" Mason asked.

"Then she got in the car and drove it away."

"How do you know she did?"

"Figure it out for yourself," Humphreys said. "I've studied the tracks carefully. This diagram shows you just what happened. She got out of the car, ran down to the road. She came back and got in the car. Fleetwood got out of the car and walked along to Overbrook's house. Those are the only tracks. The car was in soft ground. No one could have got in that car or left the car without leaving tracks. If Fleetwood had returned to the car, he'd have left tracks."

"And Overbrook's tracks?" Mason asked.

"They were made this morning. You can follow them clearly, a steady, unbroken line of tracks. He walked down from his house, just as I've shown his tracks here. He started to cut across the tracks made by the automobile, then thought better of it when he appreciated their importance, made a swing, and walked back to the farm road. Then he went and got his tractor and put the boards down."

"You don't think a person could have got to the car or left the car by carefully picking the ground, and . . ."

"Not a chance," Humphreys said. "The ground is so soft that you can even see the tracks made by Overbrook's dog when he was putting the boards down. I've just made a lot of little dots to show where those dog tracks are. I didn't sketch each individual track. But the point I'm making is that the ground is so soft that even the dog left very plain, deeply indented tracks."

"And there's no question but what these are Fleetwood's tracks?"

"None whatever. You can see them getting out of the automobile, walking around the car. There's where he stood when he looked back at Mrs. Allred. There's where he stood when he swung around and threw the gun away. There's where he resumed walking and you can follow the tracks right up to within eight or ten feet of the roadway to Overbrook's house."

Mason studied the diagram thoughtfully. "You're sure you've got everything on here?"

"Absolutely everything."

Mason said, "if this evidence is true, it's important as hell."

"It's true. The thing is right there on the ground. No person could have entered that automobile or left it without leaving tracks."

"Isn't there some way a person could have approached that automobile without leaving tracks?" Mason asked.

Humphreys shook his head doggedly.

"Not by finding some way over hard ground?"

"There wasn't any."

"Or by . . . Wait a minute," Mason said. "How about a rope? Are there overhanging tree limbs, or . . ."

"There aren't any trees there for a hundred feet. Then there are some big spreading oaks. But those trees are so far away they couldn't possibly enter into the picture. No, Mr. Mason, you can take my word for it. I looked the situation over carefully. A person couldn't possibly have entered that car or left it without leaving tracks; and the tracks I have on this map are every single track that is there on the ground. When the car drove up and stopped, there were at least two people in it. One of them was the woman who was evidently in the baggage compartment, and the other was a man who was either in the driver's seat or who got out of the car on the left-hand side where a driver would naturally alight. That man walked around the car, stood in front of the headlights and moved his feet in the position that would indicate, first, he was looking toward the back of the car, second, that he was throwing a gun away. Then he kept right on walking in a beeline for Overbrook's house. The woman came back, got in the car, and took the car away. That's the only way the car could have been taken away. That woman came back, got in the driver's seat and drove it away. The tracks tell the whole story. Whoever else was in that car when it was parked there, stayed in the car.

"You can see where the car was backed. The ground was a little soft here, and there was just a little skidding when the car backed around. Then it was driven back to the gravel surfaced road."

Mason studied the diagram, drumming with

the tips of his fingers on the edge of the desk.

"Well," Drake said, "I guess that does it, Perry."

Mason nodded.

"Of course," Mason said after a moment, "I don't suppose it's possible to check these tracks as to a means of identity. In other words, *a woman* was in the luggage compartment. This woman got out, walked to the road, turned back and returned to the car and drove it away. The tracks don't identify Mrs. Allred, merely some woman."

"Fleetwood's story identifies Mrs. Allred," Drake said.

"And Fleetwood has lied at every turn of the road so far," Mason pointed out.

"But on this angle he has corroboration," Humphreys said.

Mason said, "I don't trust that Bernice Archer, Paul. *She* might have been the one who was locked in the luggage compartment."

"Not a chance," Drake said. "Remember that Bernice Archer was in town Monday night. She got that call from the service station out by Springfield. She had a girl friend spending the night with her. They sat up and talked until about one or two in the morning and then slept together. There was only the one bed. I've checked Bernice Archer up one side and down the other. She was in her apartment all night Monday. Remember that Mrs. Allred stopped at that service station around seven o'clock and the attendant remembers her, remembers the car, and remem-

252

bers Fleetwood. Then the car went over the grade sometime around eleven o'clock. It *could* have been sometime around half past ten, probably about half an hour before the clock on the dashboard stopped and Allred's watch stopped."

"The police don't figure the car was driven over the grade at eleven o'clock when those clocks were stopped?"

"No, they figured Mrs. Allred set the clock and Allred's watch ahead so as to give herself an alibi."

Mason got up from his chair and started pacing the floor.

"You've got to take this evidence into consideration when you go before a jury," Drake said, tapping the paper.

"I know I have."

"This evidence," Drake went on, "is the controlling factor in the entire case. Whatever story your client tells, Perry, has to coincide with the evidence of these tracks."

"Her story doesn't coincide with it, Paul."

"It'll have to, by the time she gets on the witness stand."

Mason said, "If she's telling the truth, Fleetwood must have picked up some other woman, put her in the luggage compartment, had her get out, run away, return and drive the car away. If she's lying, then she's trying to protect someone. The question is — *who?*"

"Patricia," Drake said.

"Could be. But how could Patricia have been

in the luggage compartment of her mother's car? Do we know *where* she was on Monday night, Paul?"

"Apparently not."

"Find out."

"I'll try."

"Those tracks, Mr. Mason," Humphreys said. "If you can find any way of figuring how that woman could get out of that automobile after she returned, you're a better man than I am. She'd have had to have been an angel and had wings. The story is right there in the ground. She got back in the car and drove the car away."

"And Fleetwood was there at the car only that one time?"

"That's right. You can see his tracks leaving the automobile. He never returned to that car."

"Unless perhaps Overbrook is lying about the time the boards were put there," Mason said, "and . . ."

"No chance of that," Humphreys said. "I talked with Overbrook's neighbor. He saw him putting the boards down there this morning. Overbrook told him he was protecting some tracks that the sheriff might be interested in. The neighbor stood and watched him put the boards down, then drove on in to the post office. Overbrook came in just a few minutes later to telephone the sheriff."

"You've sure as hell got to adopt Fleetwood's story," Drake said. "When he finally told the truth, he made a good job of it."

254

# Chapter 18

D. T. Danvers, known to his intimates as "D. Tail" Danvers because of his passionate devotion to every small detail in a case, had been assigned by the District Attorney to the preliminary hearing of the People vs. Lola Faxon Allred.

Danvers, a chunky, thick-necked individual, aggressively determined to have his own way in a courtroom but personally friendly with the men who opposed him, paused by Mason's chair to shake hands before court opened.

"Well," he said, "I suppose this is going to be the same old runaround. You'll be sitting there making objections, trying to get us to put on just as much of our case as possible so you can stand off and snipe at it, and then when it comes to your turn, you'll fold up like a camp tent with a broken guy wire and say, 'Your Honor, I believe the State has established a sufficient case to warrant the Court in binding the defendant over, and under those circumstances I see no use in presenting any of our defense at this time.'"

Mason laughed, "What's the matter, Danvers? Were you out on a camping trip where the tent folded up?"

Judge Colton ascended the bench, said, "People versus Lola Allred. What's the situation, gentlemen?"

"The defendant is in court, defended by counsel," Danvers said, "and the prosecution is ready to go ahead."

"The defense is ready," Mason announced.

"Call your first witness," Judge Colton said.

Danvers' first witness was the doctor who had performed the autopsy on the body of Bertrand Allred. He described the man's injuries in technical terms, announced the cause of death, and gave it as his opinion that death had occurred sometime between nine o'clock and eleven-thirty o'clock Monday night.

"Cross-examine," Danvers said.

"These injuries which you have described," Mason said, "and which caused the death of the decedent — could all of them have been inflicted by means of a fall of fifty or a hundred feet while the decedent had been in an automobile?"

"With the possible exception of one blow which had been received on the skull, probably made with some circular instrument such as a gun barrel or a jack handle, or a piece of small, very heavy pipe."

"That couldn't have been caused by hitting the head in falling against some object such as the edge of the dashboard or the side of the steering wheel?"

"I don't *think* it could."

"Do you *know* that it couldn't?"

"No, I don't. Naturally, there's a certain element of surmise. The final resting place of the automobile in which the body was found was, I understand, some distance from the place where it struck the first time. Yet at the time that it first struck, there was the force of a considerable impact."

"That's all," Mason said.

A police laboratory expert testified to examining a piece of carpet, similar to that usually placed in the luggage compartments of automobiles. There were stains on this carpet which he said were human blood.

"Cross-examine," Danvers said.

"What type?" Mason asked. "What group did the blood belong to?"

"Type O."

"Do you know what type blood the defendant has?"

"She also has type O."

"Do you know what type blood the decedent, Bertrand Allred, had?"

"No, sir. I do not. I didn't classify that."

"You merely found out that the type of blood that was on this piece of carpet, which you understood came from the luggage compartment of the defendant's automobile, was of the same type as the blood of the defendant. After that you ceased to be interested or to investigate further. Is that right?"

"Well, I . . . ."

"Is it right, or isn't it?"

"No."

"Well, what *did* you do further?"

"Well, I . . . I made a careful investigation to

prove that it was blood, and then that it was human blood."

"And then you classified it?"

"Yes."

"And found out it was type O?"

"Yes, sir."

"And found out that the defendant had type O?"

"Yes."

"And don't you know, as a matter of fact, that between forty and fifty percent of the entire white race has blood of type O?"

"Well . . . yes."

"And you felt certain even before you had made the test that the result of this test would show that this blood came from the body of the defendant?"

"Not exactly."

"Then why did you type the blood of the defendant and the blood on the carpet, which you have mentioned?"

"Well, I wanted to show that it *could* have come from the defendant. Having shown that, there was nothing further that I could show."

"And you didn't type the blood of the decedent?"

"Wait a minute, I did, too. I have some notes on that. If you'll pardon me just a moment."

The witness took a notebook from his pocket, said, "The blood typing was incident to other matters and . . . yes, here it is. The decedent also had blood of type O — that isn't particularly significant because as you yourself have pointed out, between forty and fifty percent of the white population of the world has blood of this type. The idea of my tests on the matter was not to show that the blood *did* come from the defendant, but that it *could* have come from the defendant."

"And could also have come from anyone comprising fifty percent of the population."

"Yes."

"That's all," Mason said.

One of the traffic officers described inspecting the automobile with Allred's body inside, mentioned that the automobile had been locked in low gear when it went over the embankment, and apparently had been deliberately driven off the road and over the bank.

Mason asked no questions.

"Robert Fleetwood, take the stand," Danvers said.

Fleetwood was sworn, took the stand and testified, giving a full account of events leading to Allred's meeting him and Mrs. Allred at the Snug-Rest Auto Court around ten o'clock Monday evening.

"Then what happened?" Danvers asked.

"He seemed cordial enough. He was still posing as my brother-in-law. He shook hands, asked me how I was feeling and if I was regaining my memory. I said I wasn't and then Allred said we'd have to leave this court because he had much better accommodations down the road a piece.

259

"I didn't have any baggage except a razor and some toilet articles Bertrand Allred had given me. Mrs. Allred had a very small suitcase. We were able to leave the court almost at once.

"Well, he'd raised the turtleback to put Mrs. Allred's bag in there, and suddenly he whipped out a gun and ordered her to crawl in there. She refused. He hit her hard in the face, and she knew then he meant business. She crawled in. At that time I noticed her nose was bleeding."

Convincingly he went on with his story, through the overpowering of Allred and starting for the Overbrook ranch. His recital tallied almost word for word with the story he had told Tragg and Mason previously.

"Did you know Overbrook?"

"Not personally, but I knew quite a bit about him from the books. He'd had some correspondence with us over a mining deal. I knew he wouldn't sell me out to Allred."

"So what did you do?"

"Well," Fleetwood said, "I'd been pretending that I had amnesia. I thought it would be a pretty good thing to keep right on pretending. I drove the car up the road to Overbrook's property, and about a quarter of a mile before I came to the house, I turned off the road in what seemed to be a nice open spot where I could get the car off the road and leave it. It turned out to be a soft spot where there was a certain amount of drainage from high ground on either side, which, coupled with the recent rain, had left the ground quite soft, but the car went in there all right."

"In low gear?"

"In second gear, I believe."

"Then what happened?"

"I moved the car off the road and stopped it."

"Then what?"

"Mrs. Allred had evidently used a jack handle to pry back the catch on the door of the turtle-back . . ."

"You don't *know* she had used a jack handle?"

"No. All I know is that when she was put in there, the catch was shut, but when I stopped the car, she had got the catch open."

"And what happened?"

"Almost as soon as I stopped the car, she pushed up the turtleback of the car and jumped out of the luggage compartment to the ground and started to run."

"In which direction?"

"Back. Toward the road we had just left."

"Did you say anything?"

"I called to her and said, 'You don't need to run. He's knocked out. He's absolutely uncon-scious.' "

"Did she say anything?"

"No. She just kept on running."

"But your voice was loud enough so she must have heard you?"

"Sure, she heard me."

"Then what?"

"I didn't bother with her any more. I remem-bered Allred's gun that I was still holding. I threw that gun just as far as I could throw it."

"In which direction?"

"I think in a general north — well, a north-easterly direction from the car."

"Then what happened?"

"There weren't any lights in Overbrook's house, but I could hear the barking of a dog, and that guided me. I walked directly to Overbrook's house."

"Did you go back to the road?"

"No. I just hit a beeline for where the dog was barking."

"Then what happened?"

"I got Overbrook up out of bed. I asked him if he could put me up. I told him I didn't know who I was or anything about myself."

"He agreed to?"

"Yes. He gave me a bed."

"Did you go to bed?"

"Yes."

"And did you at any time during the night leave that bed?"

"No. I couldn't have. The dog was watching."

"By the dog, you mean Overbrook's dog?"

"Yes."

"Where was he?"

"In the living room."

"How do you know?"

"Because I sat up and sort of thought I'd look around. I heard the automobile start up, and wondered if Allred had regained consciousness. I tried to open the door and look out, but the dog was there and he growled."

"Wasn't there a window?"

"That's the point. The room was on the other side of the house, so I couldn't see in the direction in which I'd parked the car. I wanted to get out and look through the windows of the other room in the house."

"That was a rather simple house?"

"Yes."

"Consisting of two rooms?"

"Four rooms. There was a room where Overbrook slept, a little kitchen, a room where I was sleeping and a living room."

"Overbrook was there alone?"

"Yes. He was batching there."

"What happened after that?"

The witness grinned and said, "I was trapped by my own device. Mr. Perry Mason drove up to the house and identified me and had a girl along who claimed I was her long lost husband. There was nothing I could do about it, without showing Overbrook that I'd been lying all along about the amnesia and I wasn't in a position to do that. I still thought it would be a lot better for me to pretend that I couldn't remember anything that had happened after that blow on the head, so I went along with them."

"And what happened?"

"Mr. Mason took me to police headquarters."

"Cross-examine," Danvers said to Perry Mason.

Mason said to Danvers, "I suppose you have a

map prepared showing the place where the car was parked and all that. You're going to introduce it eventually. Why not bring it into evidence now, and give me a chance to cross-examine this witness in connection with the map."

"Very well," Danvers said, and handed Mason a map which was similar to the diagram Bert Humphreys had drawn for Paul Drake.

"We'll identify this right now, if you want, with the testimony of the surveyor who made the . . ."

"I don't think that's necessary," Mason said. "You can put the surveyor on later, but we have Fleetwood on the stand now and we may just as well finish with him."

"Very well. And here are some photos of the tracks."

"I'll call your attention to this map," Mason said, "and ask you if this seems to be a correct map or diagram showing the vicinity of Overbrook's house?"

"Yes, sir. That is."

"And where did you leave the car?"

"At this point."

"And where was the luggage compartment of the car located?"

"Right about here. Right where you see the footprints of this woman — the dots marked here as *'Woman's Footprints Running.'* You see they start here. That's where the luggage compartment was located. They run down to the road."

"And then you see a series of dots marked

'Woman's Footprints Returning'?"

"That's right."

"And what are those?"

"Well, of course, I don't *know* what they are. I think that's where Mrs. Allred and . . ."

"Never mind what you think," Danvers interrupted. "Just confine your answers to what you know, and I'll make Mr. Mason confine his questions to the issues. I object, Your Honor, to Counsel's question on the ground that it calls for a conclusion of the witness and . . ."

"The objection would have been sustained, but the question was already asked and answered."

"Not completely answered, Your Honor."

"Very well, the objection is sustained. The answer of the witness will be stricken from the record. Go ahead, Mr. Mason."

"Why," Mason asked, "didn't you complain to the police?"

"I didn't have an opportunity."

"You had an opportunity to get to a telephone and call Donnybrook 6981, didn't you?"

"Yes."

"The number of someone in whom you are interested?"

"Yes."

"And you wanted to appeal to this person for help?"

"Well, I wanted to get away from the predicament in which I found myself."

"And did you, or did you not, talk with this person at Donnybrook 6981?"

"I did not. That was the number of Miss Bernice Archer, a friend of mine."

"A close friend?"

"Yes."

"And you wanted to advise her of what was happening?"

"Yes. I didn't intend to ask her for help or to notify the police, but I didn't want her to think I skipped out with a married woman."

"You placed a call to her from a service station telephone, while Mrs. Allred was in the women's rest room at the service station?"

"Yes, sir."

"And then didn't wait for the call to be answered?"

"No, sir. There was some delay. Then Mrs. Allred came out and I didn't want her to see me at the telephone."

"That was the first opportunity you'd had to use a telephone?"

"Well, just about the first opportunity, yes."

"You were in a motel all day Sunday?"

"Yes."

"And Monday morning?"

"Yes."

"There was no phone there?"

"No, sir."

"Did you try to find a phone?"

"Yes."

"Was Mrs. Allred there all that time?"

"Not all the time, no. But she was right close. I don't think she was ever away from me over,

266

well, over ten or fifteen minutes at a time."

"You could have got up and walked out any time you wanted to?"

"Well, I guess I could have. Yes."

"You didn't want to?"

"Well, I wanted to see how the situation was going to adjust itself."

"Yet you realized that Allred might show up at any moment?"

"To tell you the truth, Mr. Mason, I didn't want to do anything that would make a scene, because I didn't want to be put in a position of having to explain my actions."

"Why not?"

"Because I thought that if I could fool everyone, and if Allred thought that I thought Patricia's car had struck the blow that knocked me out, I might turn the situation somewhat to my advantage."

"In what way?"

"I could lull Allred into a feeling of false security and have a chance to communicate with Mr. Jerome and explain matters to him."

"Had you made any attempt to communicate with Jerome?"

"Yes."

"When?"

"While we were there at the motel at Springfield."

"And what did you do?"

"I called Mr. Jerome on the phone."

"Oh you did, eh?"

"Yes, sir."

"And what did you tell him?"

"I didn't talk with him. I left a message for him. He was out."

"What did you say in this message?"

"Objected to as incompetent, irrelevant and hearsay," Danvers said. "Not proper cross-examination."

"Sustained," Judge Colton snapped.

"Now just a moment," Mason said. "Your attitude toward the defendant in this case, Mrs. Allred, is influenced in some way by your business connections?"

"Well, only in a way."

"You know that as the surviving partner, Mr. Jerome will be in charge of winding up the partnership business?"

"Well, generally, yes."

"And you expect to be employed by Mr. Jerome?"

"Objected to as incompetent, irrelevant and immaterial," Danvers said.

"I beg your pardon," Mason snapped. "This is going to the motivation of the witness, his bias, his interest in the testimony which he is giving. I am entitled to show that on cross-examination."

"You're right," Judge Colton said. "The objection is overruled."

"Well," Fleetwood said, and hesitated. "I guess I'd thought of that."

"And the real reason, the underlying reason that you didn't simply get up and walk out on Mrs. Allred there at that motel, was because you felt that at some time in the future you'd be able to turn the tables on Bertrand C. Allred and kill him, and that George Jerome with his money and his connections would stand back of you. Isn't that right?"

"No."

"Not even generally?"

"No."

"Then why didn't you simply wait until a propitious moment, smile at Mrs. Allred and say, 'I'm sorry, Mrs. Allred, but this is all an act on my part. I'm going to leave you now'?"

"Well . . . because of certain complications. I wanted to stall along until Jerome could have a chance to catch Allred red-handed. The message I left for Jerome would tell him what to do. I wanted to keep Allred occupied with me until Jerome had the evidence sewed up."

"You were then working hand-in-glove with Jerome?"

"In a way. I expected to co-operate with him, and have him co-operate with me."

"That's all," Mason said.

"No further questions. Call P. E. Overbrook."

Overbrook, attired in overalls and jumper, strode up to the stand, a big, good-natured giant, embarrassed by the crowd in the courtroom and his strange surroundings.

He took the oath, gave his name and address to the clerk, and turned uneasily to face Danvers.

"You're the P. E. Overbrook who has the property described as the Overbrook ranch? You have seen this diagram and can identify this as marking the location of your house on that diagram?"

"Yes, sir."

Mason said to Danvers, "As I understand the rule, Counselor, leading questions are permitted on direct examination when they are preliminary, merely; but I would suggest that if you don't want me to object, you had better let the witness himself testify from here on."

"My question was merely preliminary. I was trying to save time."

"You could save more time if you gave all the testimony for this witness," Mason said. "Time is important, but there are other matters more important."

Danvers grinned and said, "I'm trying to save time, and you're trying to save the defendant's neck."

"That will do, gentlemen," Judge Colton said. "Please get on with the case, Mr. Danvers."

"You've seen the witness, Fleetwood, who just testified?"

"Yes, sir."

"When did you first see him?"

"Why, he came to my place Monday night."

"About what time Monday?"

"Well, now, I can't tell. It was after I'd gone to bed, and I woke up because the dog was barking. I never looked at the watch."

"All right. What wakened you?"

"First I heard the dog bark, and then I thought I might have heard a car."

"So you were awake, then, when Fleetwood came to the house?"

"Yes, sir."

"And what happened?"

"Well, the dog barked real loud and I knew someone was right out in the yard. Then I heard someone speak to the dog and then there was the sound of knuckles on the door."

"The dog didn't bite?"

"No. The dog doesn't bite. He barks, and he runs up and smells people, and I don't know what would happen if a person tried to do something he wasn't supposed to do. But as long as a person is going directly to the house and knocking on the door, the dog just keeps on barking, and that's all."

"So you went to the door and let Fleetwood in?"

"Yes, sir."

"Then what happened?"

"Well, this man told me that he found himself wandering around, that he guessed he'd been in an automobile accident, that he didn't know who he was and couldn't remember anything about himself. So, naturally, I took him in."

"Where did you put him?"

"Well, sir, I didn't know anything at all about who he was, and thinking I might have heard a car motor stop down there made me kind of suspicious."

"You didn't say anything to this man about hearing the car stop?"

271

"No. I wasn't even certain I had heard a car. I thought I might have — and the way the dog acted I thought a car had stopped."

"Did the man tell you anything about having driven up in an automobile?"

"No. He said he just couldn't remember a thing, that he just found himself walking along the road."

"You knew that was a lie?"

"Well, to tell you the truth, I thought the guy was hot."

"So what did you do?"

"Well, it was a cold, drizzly night and I didn't want to turn him out, but I didn't want to take any chances. I had a spare room with a cot in it and some blankets were there. I told him that I ran a bachelor's place, and that he'd have to get in a bed without sheets, just some blankets."

"And what did he say?"

"He seemed tickled to death. So I put him in that room."

"And then what?"

"And then," Overbrook said with a grin, "I took Prince, that's the dog, and put him in the living room, and I told Prince to watch him and keep him in there, and then I went back to bed and went to sleep. I knew that that fellow could never get out of that room without Prince nabbing him."

"You feel absolutely certain that he didn't leave the room after he once entered it?"

Overbrook grinned and said, "When I tell

272

Prince to keep somebody in a place and to watch him, why you can gamble Prince is going to do it."

"How big a dog is Prince?"

"He weighs about eighty-five pounds. He's a lot of dog."

"Then what happened?"

"Well, then, the next day this man Mason came and there was a party with him, and a woman that said she was this man's wife, and everything seemed to be all hunky-dory, so they had a grand family reunion with a lot of billing and cooing, and this woman seemed just crazy to get her husband away from there and that was okay by me."

"In other words, you accepted everything at its face value?"

"I still thought the guy was hot," Overbrook said, "but I wasn't sticking my neck out."

"So they went away?"

"That's right."

"Then what happened?"

"Well," Overbrook said, "nothing happened, until the next morning."

"And then?"

"Well, about daylight the next morning I began doing a lot of thinking. I remembered noticing Fleetwood's tracks and I thought I'd see if I couldn't back-track him a ways."

"Now this was Wednesday morning?"

"That's right."

"So what did you do?"

"Well, I started out and picked up Fleetwood's tracks, and then I back-tracked him. I was careful not to step in his tracks. I just walked along . . ."

"On this diagram," Danvers interrupted, "there's a line of dots which are labeled FLEETWOOD'S TRACKS TO THE HOUSE."

"That's right. Those are his tracks."

"And another line of dots going in an opposite direction labeled OVERBROOK'S TRACKS FOLLOWING FLEETWOOD'S TRAIL."

"That's right."

"And those are your tracks?"

"Yes, sir."

"Now those tracks follow along parallel with the tracks left by Fleetwood?"

"Yes, sir. I back-tracked him down to where the car had stopped, and I started to circle around and then all of a sudden I seen these tracks where a woman had jumped out of the automobile and run back to the highway, and then I looked and saw a woman's tracks coming back again from the highway and getting in the automobile apparently to drive it off. So I knew I'd better call the officers. It looked like a woman had been shut up in the luggage compartment."

"So then what did you do?"

"Well, I kept right on walking to the hard ground without looking around any. You can see where these tracks of mine circle right up into the high ground up here. I have a farm road up there that runs out to my grain field."

"A farm service road?"

"Yes, sir."

"And what did you do?"

"I walked up to that road and went back to the house and kept thinking things over; so then I took my tractor and trailer and loaded on a lot of scrap lumber, so people could get out there without messing things up any, and put the lumber down."

"How did you put it down?"

"Why the way a person would put down lumber so as to save tracks that way. I'd put down a board and then walk out along that board and put down another board and then walk out along that board and put down another board until I had boards all the way out to where the car had stopped, and then I walked back along the boards, got in my tractor and drove back to my house, got my jalopy out of the shed and drove in to where there was a telephone. I called the sheriff and told him that I'd been putting up a man that said he had amnesia and I thought he might be hot and that I'd tracked him out to where he'd parked his automobile and, sure enough, I'd found there'd been a woman in the back end of the car and she'd jumped out and run down to the highway, and then after a while apparently she'd sneaked back and picked up the car and driven off."

"At that time had you heard of Allred's death?"

"No, sir. I hadn't."

"Cross-examine," Danvers said.

Mason smiled reassuringly at the witness.

"So Fleetwood came to your place on Monday night and was there until sometime Tuesday?"

"That's right; until you came and got him."

"During that time he stayed in the house?"

"Not all of the time."

"You didn't stay in the house?"

"Me? No. I was out around the place doing chores."

"You left Fleetwood alone there?"

"Some of the time, yes."

"Fleetwood could have walked away and gone anywhere he wanted to?"

"Sure."

"You didn't tell the dog to guard him then?"

"No, the dog was with me."

"You and the dog are quite close?"

"I'm fond of him and he's fond of me."

"He accompanies you wherever you go?"

"Everywhere," Overbrook said, "except when I've got some job for him to do like watching somebody or something. Aside from that, my dog's with me all the time."

"The dog is loyal to you and devoted?"

"Yes."

"And you could have left him to watch Fleetwood and the dog would have kept him there?"

"Sure, but I couldn't have done it without Fleetwood knowing what I was doing."

"And you didn't want to do that?"

"It didn't seem exactly hospitable."

"Weren't you afraid Fleetwood would steal something and . . ."

Overbrook's grin was slow and good-natured. "Mr. Mason," he said, "the stuff I got out in my cabin isn't the stuff a man like Fleetwood would steal. I've got a little bacon and some flour and a little salt and some baking powder. I have some blankets and some cots to put 'em on, but — well, Mr. Mason there isn't anything there for anybody to steal. I live kind of simple, myself."

Mason said, "It didn't occur to you to back-track Fleetwood to see where he came from until Wednesday morning?"

"Well, I just kept thinking things over all the time. Things kept churning around in my mind and I couldn't get them straightened out. The way you folks had showed up and taken this man away with you, and all this stuff, I just couldn't get the thing out of my mind. So I started looking around and then just as soon as I seen the tracks made by this woman — you could see she was running."

"Even without walking over to where the tracks were?"

"Yes, sir. People that live out in the country the way I do get so they're pretty good at telling things about tracks, and the minute I saw these tracks, even without walking over to them, I could see that a woman had got out of that automobile and had really high-tailed it down the road; and then I saw where she'd come back and she was walking slow and easy like when she came back. So I decided I'd just better tell the sheriff about the thing."

"So then what did you do?"

"Just what I told you."

"Now, would it have been possible for any person to have gone out to that automobile without leaving tracks?"

"Not in the ground that's around that automobile. No, sir. There's kind of a seepage there and the ground is nearly always soft for quite a little while after a rain."

"Did you find the gun?"

"Yes, sir, I did."

"When?"

"Well, that was after the sheriff got out there and we looked the tracks over a bit and the sheriff asked me to tell him what I could about them, and I noticed the tracks made by this man Fleetwood when he got out from behind the steering wheel of the automobile and walked around the front of the car. I could tell from those tracks that about the time he got even with the headlights, he'd turned around and done something, and the way the right foot was sort of smudged, I figured that he'd heaved something or thrown something and told the sheriff about it. So, the sheriff and I, we went out in the hard ground and started looking around and found it. It just happened I was the one that found the gun."

"And what happened? Did you pick it up?"

"Not me," Overbrook said, grinning. "I'd read enough detective stories so I know about fingerprints. I just called the sheriff and told him the gun was over there, and the sheriff didn't pick it up. Not then. We got a stake and drove it into the ground where the gun was lying, and then the sheriff got a piece of string and slipped it through the trigger guard on the gun and pulled it up so he didn't touch it. That way we didn't smudge any fingerprints that were on it. I heard afterwards that they'd found . . ."

"Never mind what you'd heard," Danvers said, interrupting. "Just tell Mr. Mason the facts."

"Yes, sir."

"I think that's all," Mason said.

"That's our case, Your Honor," Danvers said.

"You're resting?" Mason asked, with some surprise.

"Certainly," Danvers said.

"I move that the Court dismiss the case and free the defendant from custody," Mason said. "There is no evidence sufficient to show that she is in any way connected with what happened."

"On the contrary," Danvers said. "There's every evidence. We have to go through with this every time, Your Honor, but I suppose I may as well point out for the sake of the record what we have. We now have the testimony of witnesses showing that Allred was unconscious in an automobile, that Mrs. Allred was in the luggage compartment of that automobile. These tracks can't lie. The person who was in the luggage compartment of that automobile got out and ran to the highway. Then after a while she turned around and walked back to the car, got in it and drove away. The unconscious form of her husband was in the car at that time. He couldn't have recovered consciousness and left the car without leaving tracks. You can see from this diagram of tracks where the car was backed, turned and driven back to the roadway, headed in the direction of the main mountain road.

"I have a lot of other evidence that I *can* introduce, but the object of the defense counsel at this time is to force me to show all of my hand without showing any of his, and then when the case comes up for trial in the superior court, he will be in a position to have me at just that much of a disadvantage.

"The only object of this preliminary hearing is to prove that a crime has been committed, and to show there is reasonable ground for believing that the defendant committed that crime. I claim I have abundantly met the requirements of the law."

"I think so," Judge Colton said. "The motion is denied. Does the defense have any evidence at all it wishes to introduce?"

Mason said, "I notice that George Jerome is in court, and yet he was not called as a witness."

"I didn't need him."

"I'll call him as my witness," Mason said.

"Now then, Your Honor," Danvers protested. "This is an old trick, and it's just a trick. The lawyer for the defense knows that his client is going to get bound over, so he doesn't care what happens in this court. He isn't bound by it. Therefore, he calls people and goes on fishing expeditions and . . . ."

"I understand the basic rules of courtroom tactics," Judge Colton said, smiling, "but I don't think you would claim, Counselor, that Mr. Mason does not have a right to call any person whom he wishes as a witness."

"No, Your Honor, but I do want to point out that George Jerome will be a prosecution witness and, in the event Mr. Mason puts him on the stand, I want Counsel to be confined to the examination of this witness according to the strict rules of evidence. I don't want him to start cross-examining the witness."

"When and if that happens, you may object," Judge Colton said. "In the meantime, George Jerome is called to the stand as a witness for the defense."

Jerome was sworn, looked somewhat angrily at Mason as he settled his huge frame there on the witness stand.

"Your name is George Jerome. You're a partner, or were a partner, of Bertrand C. Allred?"

"Yes, sir."

"You were, of course, quite well acquainted with Allred during his lifetime?"

"Yes."

"When was the last time you saw him alive?"

"Objected to as incompetent, irrelevant and immaterial," Danvers said.

"Overruled."

"Well, it was, let me see. It was Monday evening

281

about — oh about half-past six o'clock, I'd say."

"Where?"

"Now you mean the *last* time I saw him?"

"Yes."

"Well, it was out at his house. That is, out at the part of the house he calls his office — the place he has set aside for his office work."

"That was Monday evening, the night of the murder?" Mason asked.

"Yes, sir."

"What did you talk about?"

"Objected to, if the Court please, as incompetent, irrelevant and immaterial."

"Sustained."

"Was anyone else there with you at that time?"

"No, sir."

"Now when you drove away from that house did you take Mr. Allred with you?"

"Yes, sir. I did."

"In the automobile with you?"

"Yes, sir."

"You took him up to the Snug-Rest Auto Court, didn't you?"

"Objected to as leading and suggestive."

"Sustained."

"Where did you take him?"

"To a car rental place on Seventh Street."

"Then what did you do?"

"I stopped the car and let him out."

"Did Mr. Allred tell you why he wanted you to take him there?"

"He said he wanted to rent a car."

"Did he say where he wanted to go in that car?"

"No, sir."

Paul Drake, pushing his way through the spectators, opened the gate in the mahogany railing which separated the bar from the spectators, tiptoed to Mason's side and whispered, "I've just found out, Perry, that the D. A.'s office knows all about how Allred got to the Snug-Rest. He rented a car and driver to take him up there. He got there between nine-thirty and ten-thirty, the driver isn't certain of the time. Of course, that doesn't help you any because, while it corroborates Mrs. Allred's story, it also ties right in with Fleetwood's story."

"Thanks," Mason said in a whisper.

The lawyer turned to Jerome. "Mr. Jerome, you knew where Mr. Allred was going, didn't you?"

"No, sir."

"But you surmised it?"

"Objected to as argumentative, as an attempt to cross-examine his own witness," Danvers said.

"Of course," Mason pointed out to the Court, "this is a hostile witness and . . ."

"The Court understands," Judge Colton interrupted. "If you want to assure the Court that this is your witness and you are calling him to prove some specific point which you can state to the Court, the situation will then be different. As matters now stand, this is merely a fishing expedition with one of the prosecution's witnesses, and the Court will hold you to strict rules of procedure on direct examination. I take it, Mr. Mason, that you are not prepared to make any statement to the Court and Counsel of what you expect to prove by this witness?"

"No, Your Honor."

"I thought not."

"But," Mason said, turning again to the witness, "you did follow Mr. Allred, didn't you?"

"Objected to as leading and suggestive."

"Sustained."

"Were you at any time on Monday night in the vicinity of the Snug-Rest Auto Court?"

"Objected to as incompetent, irrelevant and immaterial. No proper foundation laid."

"Sustained."

"When was the last time you saw Bertrand Allred alive?"

"Objected to as already asked and answered."

"Sustained."

"When was the last time you talked with Robert Fleetwood before Allred's death?"

"I can't remember."

"Did you talk with Fleetwood at any time on Monday?"

"I can't remember."

"Did you receive any message on Monday which had been left for you by Fleetwood?"

"Objected to as assuming a fact not in evidence, and attempting to cross-examine his own witness."

Judge Colton said, "Mr. Mason, before I rule on that objection, I want to reiterate the position of the Court, which is that of being opposed to fishing expeditions by Counsel. Now, if you have reason to believe . . ."

"I do, Your Honor. The witness, Fleetwood, has stated that he did leave a message for this witness."

"Very well, the objection is overruled. Answer the question."

Jerome said, "I received a message which I was told had been left for me by Fleetwood. It said not to make any settlement with Allred until I had talked with Fleetwood."

"And when you talked with Fleetwood, what did he tell you?"

"Objected to as hearsay, incompetent, irrelevant and immaterial."

"Sustained."

Judge Colton said, "I wish to call to the attention of Counsel that my position on all of these questions will be the same. If Counsel can state to the Court that he is prepared to prove some specific fact by this witness, there will be a great deal more leniency in connection with the examination of this witness.

"However," Judge Colton went on, "it seems that we have reached the noon hour, and the Court will adjourn until two o'clock this afternoon. The defendant, in the meantime, is remanded to the custody of the sheriff. That's all, Mr. Jerome. You will leave the witness stand and return at two o'clock this afternoon for further examination. Court's adjourned."

Mrs. Allred leaned over and touched Mason's arm. "I want to talk with you," she said tensely.

Mason said to the deputy sheriff, "My client wants to confer with me. May I have a few minutes?"

"Okay," the deputy said. "Not too long."

Mason nodded, took Mrs. Allred's arm and escorted her over to a corner of the courtroom. "What is it?" he asked.

She said, "It's the truth, Mr. Mason."

"What is?"

"What Fleetwood has said."

"You mean you *were* in the turtleback of that automobile?"

"Yes."

Mason said grimly, "This is a hell of a time to say so."

"I can't help it, Mr. Mason. I had Pat to think of."

"What about Pat? What does she have to do with it?"

"Nothing, Mr. Mason. Nothing at all. Now don't misunderstand me. Please don't misunderstand me on that. That would be the last straw."

"I was merely taking what you said at its face value."

"No, no. When I said I had to protect Pat, I meant that I felt it would be bad for her if I should admit I'd driven that automobile over the grade. I — well, that was what was in my mind all along — to try and avoid putting Pat in an embarrassing position."

Mason said, "Well, suppose you try telling me the truth for a change. Just what did happen?"

"It was *almost* the way Bob Fleetwood said. He did drive the automobile off the road and stop, and I got out and ran down to the road. He called to me and told me that my husband was unconscious. I stopped then, and I saw him standing in front of the headlights. I saw him throw a gun just as far as he could throw it out into the darkness. And then I saw him turn and walk away from the automobile."

"I think it was because he threw away that gun that I was convinced. I knew he never in the world would have done that if my husband hadn't been unable to hurt him. And, the way he did it, made me think that — well, you know, there was a certain gesture of finality about it. So I turned around and tiptoed back to the car and peeked inside to see just what the situation was.

"Bertrand was slumped over in a corner of the car, utterly motionless. You couldn't hear a sound."

"Fleetwood said he was breathing very heavily," Mason said.

"Fleetwood is lying about that. My husband was dead."

"You're certain?"

"I should be certain. I stood there for a moment by the door of the car. Then I put my foot on the running board, raised myself up and said, 'Bertrand.' He made no answer. I leaned over and felt of his wrist. It had that peculiar clammy

287

feeling that tells its own story. But I wanted to make sure. I felt of his pulse. He was dead."

"Then why didn't you go back and call the police?"

She said, "I didn't realize the situation in which I'd placed myself until after I'd entered the automobile. I realized then that the ground was so soft that every single track showed.

"Bob Fleetwood is right about one thing. After I got in the luggage compartment, I lay there for a while, very cramped in that small space. Then I remembered we always kept an electric lantern in there for use in case of an emergency in changing tires. I found the electric lantern and switched it on. By examining the catch, I felt sure I could pry the catch back and get the lid of the luggage compartment open if I had a lever of some sort. Then I thought of the jack handle. I found that and tried it. It was pretty hard to manipulate things while the car was moving over the road, particularly that dirt road. It was a little rough.

"However, I finally got the catch back and got the lid so I could raise it. I was just in the act of raising the lid when the car turned off the road and stopped. I pushed the cover of the luggage compartment up far enough to get out, and jumped to the ground. I heard the lid bang down behind me, and I started running.

"I don't think I'd gone over thirty or forty feet when I heard Bob Fleetwood call out that everything was all right and not to worry; that Bertrand was unconscious.

"I kept right on running, but I looked back over my shoulder and saw Bob Fleetwood throw the gun away. Then he walked away from the car. And, as I told you, I returned to the car and found my husband was dead.

"It wasn't until that time I realized that from the nature of the ground in which the car was sitting my tracks showed. They showed just exactly what I had done, and I knew that if I left tracks going back to the automobile, then leaving the automobile and going back to the road again, it would look as though I had returned to kill my husband with the jack handle.

"So I thought I'd drive the car to some place where the ground was firmer, where I could get out without leaving tracks. Then I got the idea, why not drive the car off the grade and make it look as though my husband had lost control of the car?

"Well, I did that, and that was when I got the idea of pretending that Bob had stolen my car. I thought that would pass the buck to him, and then if anything turned up, in order to save his own skin, he'd have to say that he killed Bertrand in self-defense, I . . . well, I guess I didn't do a very good job of thinking, but I'd been through a lot that night, Mr. Mason."

Mason said, "Is this the truth?"

"It's the truth."

"Look at me."

She met his eyes.

"If I'd known this a long while ago," Mason

said, "I could probably have tied the killing to Bob Fleetwood. As it is now, you've lied and Fleetwood has lied. A judge or jury will have to toss up to decide which is telling the truth.

"The fact that Fleetwood threw the gun away makes me feel your husband was dead when Fleetwood left the car, but because you lied at the start, you've given Fleetwood all the trumps to play against us."

"I'm sorry, Mr. Mason."

"Look here, is this the truth?"

"Yes."

Mason said, "If you are changing your story simply because you think Fleetwood's testimony has given you a good chance to crawl out from under, you're a fool."

"No, I'm not just changing my story. I'm — I have Pat to think of . . . I . . ."

She started to sob.

Mason said, "Well, I'm not going to let you change your story. I'm not going to let you tell *any* story for a while. You aren't to talk with anyone — *anyone*. Do you understand that?"

"Yes."

"And don't ever forget, a good lie can sometimes have all the grace of artistry, but only the truth can have the ring of sincerity."

And Mason raised his hand, beckoned to the deputy.

# Chapter 19

Mason, Della Street and Paul Drake sat at a luncheon table in a restaurant at the country town where John Colton was presiding over the preliminary investigation.

"Well," Mason said, "at this late date, my client tells me another story, Paul."

"The same thing that Fleetwood says?"

"Just about. She says her husband was dead when she entered the car after Fleetwood had left it. If she's telling the truth on that, I don't know how I'm ever going to get a jury to believe her."

"I'd say that Allred must have been dead when Fleetwood threw the gun away," Drake said. "Otherwise, Fleetwood would hardly have thrown the gun. That's the act of a man who is trying to get rid of a murder weapon. He'd struck Allred on the head hard enough to kill him, and he knew it. The weapon he used had been the barrel of the gun, and when he threw the gun away it was a very natural, logical, and typical effort on the part of a murderer to get rid of the murder weapon."

"I know," Mason said, "but I don't know whether a jury will know. In all probability, the other way is better. If it's the truth."

"What other way?" Drake asked.

"Make the jury realize the character of Bertrand

Allred. Let the jury feel that Allred was still alive when his wife got in the car; that she started to drive him home; that Allred regained consciousness and started struggling with her, trying to overpower her; that she hit him then and killed him in self-defense."

"You could make quite a case that way," Drake said.

"It's a case that would appeal to the sympathies of the jurors all right, particularly in view of Fleetwood's testimony. But what bothers me is that I can't be certain it's the truth. Mrs. Allred may be trying to climb aboard and ride along on Fleetwood's story."

"Well, what do you care? Fleetwood has to give her a free ride — now."

"But I'm afraid to have her tie to something unless it's the truth. Believe me, Paul, when you're in a jam the truth is the only thing solid enough and substantial enough to rely on."

"Of course, your client hasn't been on the stand yet," Drake pointed out. "The only one she's told her story to is you."

Mason said, "I'd like to reopen the case. I'd like to cross-examine Fleetwood a little more in detail about his reason for throwing the gun away, and just what he was trying to accomplish. And yet, there was something about the whole story . . ." Mason pushed the lunch dishes to one side, took the diagram Humphreys had made from his pocket and spread it on the table. He carefully studied the tracks.

"It's mathematical," Drake said. "That part of Fleetwood's story *has* to be true. It's corroborated by his tracks."

Mason, studying the diagram Humphreys had given him, suddenly began to chuckle.

"What is it?" Drake asked.

"Darned if I know, Paul," the lawyer said, "but I have an idea germinating in my mind. There's a very strong possibility that Mrs. Allred is still lying to me."

"You mean now?"

"Right now. That her *present* story is false."

"But why would she do that?"

"Because Fleetwood has told such a damn good lie that she thinks there's no use trying to fight against it, and because by corroborating Fleetwood's story she stands a better chance of getting the sympathy of a jury than by telling the truth, which no one will believe."

"What is the truth?" Della Street asked.

"That," Mason said, "is something I propose to find out after lunch."

# Chapter 20

Court reconvened at two o'clock. Judge Colton said, "Mr. Jerome, you were on the witness stand being examined when Court adjourned. Will you take the stand again, please. Gentlemen, the defendant is in court, the witness Jerome is on the stand. Will you please proceed with your examination, Mr. Mason?"

Mason said to Judge Colton, "Your Honor, there has been a rather unexpected development in the case. Under the circumstances, I feel that I should be permitted to recall the witness Overbrook for further cross-examination."

"I object to that, Your Honor," Danvers said. "Counsel had every opportunity to cross-examine Overbrook, and he certainly took advantage of that opportunity. He asked Overbrook searching questions and . . ."

Judge Colton nodded, said, "I would think so, yes."

Mason said desperately, "Your Honor, I can now state that I am not on a fishing expedition. If I can be permitted to cross-examine Overbrook again I feel I can bring out a point which will exonerate this defendant and definitely refute Fleetwood's testimony."

"You feel you can do that?" Judge Colton asked.

"I do, Your Honor."

"That makes the situation materially different," the judge said.

"Of course, Your Honor, I have already closed the case of the prosecution," Danvers said. "The prosecution's case is completed. It is closed."

"And," Judge Colton said grimly, "if the Court should intimate that it didn't consider the evidence sufficient to bind the defendant over, you'd be on your feet in a minute stating that you had additional evidence and asking for permission to reopen your case."

Danvers said nothing.

"Take the stand, Mr. Overbrook," Judge Colton said.

Overbrook once more took the stand.

Mason said, "You qualified, in a way, as an expert on tracks, Mr. Overbrook."

"Well, us people that live out in the country know something about tracks."

"You've done quite a bit of tracking?"

"Yes."

"And you are fairly expert on tracks?"

"Yes, sir!"

"Now, then," Mason said, "inasmuch as you seem to be an expert on tracks, will you kindly tell the Court how you know that the tracks made by this woman were tracks made by a woman jumping *from* the car and running to the highway and then coming back *to* the car?"

"Why, you can see it plain as day. Look at this here diagram. That shows you the tracks."

"Yes, that's quite true. It shows tracks leading away from the automobile and coming back to the automobile."

"Yes, sir."

"And how do you know what happened there?"

"Why, you can see it written right on the ground. No person could have got out of the automobile without leaving tracks, and no person could have got in the automobile without leaving tracks. The way these tracks are, the woman jumped out of the baggage compartment and ran down to the road and then she came back and got in the car, and the only way on earth she could have got away from there was to have driven that car away, unless she had wings. Otherwise, she would have left tracks on leaving the car."

"But there *are* tracks leaving the car," Mason said.

"What?"

"There are tracks leaving the car."

"No there ain't. I looked that ground all over and this here diagram is correct."

"But those are the tracks leaving the car," Mason said, pointing to the diagram.

"Oh, sure. Those are her tracks leaving the car the first time, before she came back to it."

"How do you know they were *before she came back?*" Mason asked. "How do you know that these tracks weren't made first, the ones coming back from the highway and going to the car? How do you know this woman didn't walk from the highway out to this point and then jump down over to this point on the ground and run back to the highway?"

"Why, now, you just can't tell for sure!" Overbrook grinned. "Except, of course, that when she made these tracks here, you can see where she got in the car. Now after she got in the car, perhaps you can tell me how she managed to get down inside the baggage compartment."

The courtroom tittered.

Judge Colton rapped with his gavel to silence the spectators.

"But suppose," Mason said, "that when those tracks were made, *the car wasn't there.*"

"Huh?" Overbrook asked, stiffening to startled attention.

Mason smiled and said, "Those tracks, Mr. Overbrook, could well have been made when the car wasn't there. It would have been a simple matter for any woman to have walked out from the roadway to the point where the car tracks were located, to have made tracks at a point even with the place where the left-hand door of the car had been, and then, by using a pole similar to the manner in which a pole vaulter makes a long leap, to have made a short jump over to this point and then *run* back to the highway."

"Well, now," Overbrook said, scratching his head, "you've got something there, Mr. Mason! There isn't anything that shows *when* the tracks were made."

"Then, by that same sign," Mason said, "there

isn't anything that shows when *your* tracks were made."

"What do you mean?"

"Your tracks, down as far as the left-hand door of the car, could have been made on Monday night," Mason said. "And then you could have gone out on your farm road Wednesday morning, put down the boards and walked out on those boards until you were in a position that was exactly even with the place where the tracks you had made Monday night ended, and then by walking back toward the farm road, your tracks would show as an uninterrupted line indicating you had made no pause. Your tracks of Wednesday could have been tacked onto your tracks of Monday. You can't prove when your own tracks were made."

"Well, of course," Overbrook said, "I didn't tie an alarm clock on each one of my tracks."

Some of the spectators in the courtroom laughed.

"No," Mason said, "but there is one very interesting thing that is shown in this photograph I am holding in my hand, but which is not shown in the diagram."

"What's that?"

"I notice," Mason said, "that these little tracks here evidently indicate the tracks made by your dog. Now then, will you kindly explain to the Court how it happens that the dog accompanied you when these tracks were made from the car to the road, but *didn't* accompany you when the tracks were made *from your house to the place where the car was parked?*"

Overbrook shifted his position in the witness chair.

"Can't you answer that question?" Mason asked.

"Well, I'm just trying to figure out an answer."

"The answer," Mason said, "is that when you made those tracks from the house to where the car was parked, you didn't have your dog with you; and the only time you didn't have your dog with you was when he had been left in the house to guard the witness Fleetwood, and that was on Monday night. Therefore, Mr. Overbrook, you made those tracks Monday night after you had put Fleetwood to bed. You left the dog to guard him, and you took a flashlight and went out to backtrack him and see what had happened at an automobile you had heard drive off the road. You got to the automobile and found a man lying in it in an unconscious condition. That man was Bertrand C. Allred, a man whom you hated because he had swindled you in a mining deal. You saw an opportunity to even the score with him and you simply got in the car, drove the car away and ran it over a grade where you knew he would be killed. Then a day or so later you began to be worried about the question of tracks and decided you'd better do something about them. So you went out and laid the boards down and finished making your tracks in an unbroken line from your house to the hard surface ground. But when you took those boards out, you were surprised to find additional tracks. Tracks had been made by some woman so that it looked as though she had jumped out of the baggage compartment and then returned to the car. Now, isn't that exactly what happened?"

"Your Honor, I object," Danvers shouted. "That question is incompetent, irrelevant, immaterial. It's not proper cross-examination and . . ."

"You look at the witness' face, young man," Judge Colton said sternly, "and you'll find that it certainly *is* competent, relevant and material. The objection is overruled. Now if you want to get at the *facts* in this case, Mr. Assistant District Attorney, the court suggests you'd better pay more attention to Mr. Mason's questions and the answers of this witness. Go ahead, Mr. Overbrook, you answer that question."

Overbrook squirmed and twisted on the witness stand as though the chair had suddenly become hot.

"Answer the question," Judge Colton said.

"Well, Your Honor," Overbrook blurted, "I'll tell you the truth. In some ways that's just about what happened. It ain't true in some respects."

"In what respects?" Mason asked.

"When I got to the car," Overbrook said, "I put my flashlight inside and saw this man in there and he was dead, and then I recognized that it was Allred, and I knew that I was in a jam because people knew I hated his guts and it would look as though — well, it would look pretty bad for me having his body found on my property, and this chap that was up there at the house, of course, he could claim that he didn't know anything about it. Well, I was in a spot. So I took the car and drove her back down to the highway and just shoved her off the cliff, and then I walked back home. I got back about maybe three or four o'clock in the morning. Of course, the dog didn't make any commotion when I slipped in, and I went to bed.

"And then Tuesday night I got to worrying about the tracks. I knew that sooner or later they'd come up there and start looking for tracks on account of this man Fleetwood having been found up at my place, and particularly after these people came and got him, so — well, you're right about what happened. I went out there Wednesday and put the boards down and finished making my string of tracks so they looked as though I'd kept right on agoing; and then I told the sheriff I'd made all the tracks Wednesday morning and nobody thought about the dog. The sheriff didn't think about it, and by gum I didn't think about it!"

Mason turned to Danvers with a grin and said, "And now, Mr. Danvers, this is your case and your witness. What do you want to do?"

"I want the case continued," Danvers said.

"Until when?" Judge Colton asked.

"Make it a — oh make it until four o'clock this afternoon, Your Honor."

"Very well," Judge Colton said, "and the Court

301

will order this witness into custody. Silence in the court! Will the spectators please cease this uproar! There is no occasion for applause. This is a court of justice. The Court will clear the courtroom . . . will the spectators please cease applauding!"

# Chapter 21

Perry Mason, his long legs elevated so that his feet rested on the corner of the desk, tilted back in his swivel chair and grinned at Paul Drake.

"You know, Paul," he said, "the possible significance of those tracks never occurred to me until after I started studying them at lunch. That's the bad part of circumstantial evidence. It can really trick you and trap you.

"I told you that Bernice Archer was a smooth individual. Tragg let her talk with Fleetwood up there in the jail, and the minute she knew what had happened she told Fleetwood to insist that Mrs. Allred had been in the luggage compartment of the automobile. She made Fleetwood tell her where the automobile had been parked and she jumped in her car and drove up there and by daylight Wednesday morning she had left tracks which would substantiate Fleetwood's story. And it was such a cinch to do. All she needed to do was to take any kind of a short pole, walk slowly from the highway out to where the automobile had been parked, then put the pole in the ground to steady her and give her leverage to jump down to a place about where the luggage compartment of the automobile would have been, and then run back to the roadway. When she did that, she didn't notice Overbrook's tracks coming out to

303

the automobile and stopping. If she had, she could have pinned the murder on Overbrook right then."

"Well who the devil *did* kill him?" Drake asked.

Mason grinned. "Now, Paul, don't start taking on the duties of the police. It's up to the police to decide that. The only thing we're supposed to do is get Mrs. Allred off."

"Well who do you *think* killed him?"

Mason said, "When Overbrook went out to investigate on Monday night, he must have had some weapon with him. He evidently didn't have a gun. He's a big, strong, powerful giant of a man and he had some sort of a club, probably a jack handle. I have an idea that Allred had regained consciousness by the time Overbrook got there, that he was probably moaning, that Overbrook got in the car, backed it down to the roadway and started to go to a doctor, that somewhere along the line he discovered the identity of his passenger and then there were words, accusations and perhaps Allred made a grab at Overbrook. Overbrook cracked him over the head."

"How do you deduce all this?"

"Because of the blood in the luggage compartment," Mason said. "No story so far has accounted for that blood. Bernice Archer was smart enough to know that the first person to tell a story that would account for that blood would have the inside track, so she deliberately made up a story for Fleetwood to tell and then went out and made tracks to substantiate that story.

"She was so anxious to have a fall guy for the police that she gilded the lily. But the minute Fleetwood told a story that accounted for the bloodstains and had tracks that would back it up he became the fair-haired boy child of the police.

"If she'd kept out of it, the tracks would eventually have given Fleetwood an out, but she couldn't realize that. Neither one of them realized what perfect tracking conditions existed at the spot where the car was parked.

"When Bernice went out there she only hoped to be able to make some significant tracks to back up Fleetwood's story. When she found what she had to work with, she really went to town.

"Now I claim that if that blood didn't come from Mrs. Allred's bloody nose, it must have come from a wound in Allred's head. I think that Overbrook became panic-stricken when he realized what he had done and started to conceal the body by putting it in the luggage compartment. Then he realized that wouldn't do him any good, and then he got the idea of taking the body out and putting it in the front of the car and driving the car over the grade."

"Why couldn't it have been Fleetwood who put the body in there?"

"Because," Mason said, "Allred weighed about a hundred and seventy-five pounds. Fleetwood is rather a slender chap and not particularly strong. Overbrook is the strong, husky farmer who could have handled a body like that without much trouble. But as far as I'm concerned, it's up to the police to worry about that. They've laid an egg, and they can hatch it."

Drake chuckled.

"How about the forged check?" Della Street asked.

"That," Mason said, "is an interesting case of where Allred really outsmarted himself.

"You can see what Allred planned to do. He intended to get Fleetwood out with his wife and then kill them both and run the car over a mountain precipice. He had a perfect scheme there. All he had to do was to keep his wife out with Fleetwood until tongues began to wag, and then let the bodies of the guilty lovers be found in the bottom of a deep canyon.

"Now Mrs. Allred wanted me to protect Pat. Her husband didn't want me messing around in the case. He wanted to have a free hand. He talked her into destroying the letter she had written me, but she was still going to send the check.

"So Allred got a bright idea. Why not keep me from getting to work on the case by seeing that I had *two* checks. One of them could be forged. He felt certain that when I got *two* checks in the same amount I'd refrain from doing anything until I could get in touch with Mrs. Allred.

"And Allred felt he only needed just one day's time. By Monday night it would be all over. And if he could fog the issues so the check Mrs. Allred sent me wasn't cashed on Monday, it would never be cashed then because a person's death automatically cancels any outstanding checks.

"Mrs. Allred had hurriedly typed the letter to the bank at Las Olitas. It was lying there on the table by her typewriter and checkbook. Allred slipped a sheet of carbon paper underneath it, traced the signature with a pointed instrument, perhaps the point of a nail file, on a check and made out the body of the check after Mrs. Allred had left. Remember, he didn't go to Springfield *with* them, but followed them after a few minutes.

"He made his wife believe that Patricia Faxon had run into Fleetwood with her automobile. You can follow Allred's reasoning all the way through. He wanted to murder Fleetwood and he made two attempts at it. He thought he had killed Fleetwood the first time when he slugged him with a club and left him lying by the hedge.

"Alfred ran along the side of the hedge when Fleetwood started to leave the place. He was waiting on the street side of the hedge, just as Fleetwood came out on the patio side at the opening by the driveway. It only took one good, heavy blow to crumple Fleetwood to the ground. Allred thought he had killed him. Then Allred dragged the body back a little ways, took his own car and parked it in such a position that when Patricia came driving up, it was almost certain that she would cut a corner of the hedge. Even if she hadn't, Allred could have gone out and crumpled the fender after the car was in the garage and then had Patricia thinking she had struck Fleetwood with that fender as she made the turn.

"Then Fleetwood regained consciousness.

307

That meant Allred had to work out some other bulletproof murder scheme. When Fleetwood pretended amnesia, Allred saw another opportunity. He got Fleetwood to go with Mrs. Allred, Mrs. Allred telling Fleetwood she was his married sister, and Allred coming to me and saying that Fleetwood had run away with his wife."

"Allred certainly went in for complicated schemes," Drake said.

"He schemed himself right into a grave," Mason said. "Evidently he hired a car and driver to take him to the Snug-Rest Auto Court and just about the time he was getting there, Fleetwood must have been trying for a getaway.

"Allred had a gun and he forced Fleetwood to stop the car and let him in. From that point on, Fleetwood's story could be the truth. The only part about it that's a lie is the story about Mrs. Allred's being in the luggage compartment. And Fleetwood and Bernice Archer hatched up that story to account for the bloodstains on the carpet of the luggage compartment."

"And Mrs. Allred changed her story to you because she felt that was her best way out?" Della Street asked.

"Sure. Fleetwood and his girl, Bernice Archer, made such a convincing story that Mrs. Allred suddenly realized she stood a better chance of going free by falling in with their story than by trying to tell the truth. The artistic way Bernice fixed up the story was that it gave Mrs. Allred almost a perfect out on a plea of self-defense —

and, of course, it got Fleetwood out of a jam.

"Circumstantial evidence never lies, but it isn't always easy to interpret it correctly."

"Well, all's well that ends well," Della Street said. "This case certainly expanded into a lot of complications from a forged check. I suppose it was that check which really aroused your suspicions, Chief."

Mason smiled. "The thing which really made me suspicious was the stories everyone had about the lazy lover. The picture of Fleetwood eloping with Mrs. Allred and then sitting back and letting her do all the running around and registering at the motel while he sat in the car, too lazy to move. Well, somehow when that picture was sketched I began to think Allred might have something up his sleeve in the way of a whole deck of marked cards."

"That's a good way to file it," Della Street said smiling, "The Case of the Lazy Lover."

We hope you have enjoyed this Large Print book. Other G.K. Hall & Co. or Chivers Press Large Print books are available at your library or directly from the publishers.

For more information about current and upcoming titles, please call or write, without obligation, to:

G.K. Hall & Co.
P.O. Box 159
Thorndike, Maine 04986 USA
Tel. (800) 257-5157

OR

Chivers Press Limited
Windsor Bridge Road
Bath BA2 3AX
England
Tel. (0225) 335336

All our Large Print titles are designed for easy reading, and all our books are made to last.